G000122819

Life of

Maggot

By Paul Jameson

Rebecca, Kit, and Finty

To t' Moon,

And Back,

Forever and Always.

Preface
On Writing and Illustrations

LIFE OF MAGGOT came upon me quite unexpected. A surprising visitor, so to speak, but one whose visit was thoroughly enjoyed. I was struggling with a piece I feared dawdled too much into the Otherworld, and so it was I took a break, whereupon Maggot raised a tiny head. At the time 'Nightjar' was receiving a lot of attention, wonderful reviews, and with readers wondering about the apocalyptic events that must have happened to create the world we find Nightjar in. Maggot gave me chance to explore these questions, albeit to his own rules; rules that incorporated use of medieval and historic images. Guided by Maggot, and as a scribe, it was as if the narrative and historic images began to dance hand in hand. If the story developed and no medieval or historic image could be found to support such direction, then that narrative was abandoned. Similarly, images or illustrations might be found online or in reading that would inspire and inform how the story was to develop. In an artistic sense it was somewhat akin to being blown in the wind, an experience I thoroughly enjoyed. All being said and done though, there are still many features of the tale that will help readers knit Maggot into the same universe as Nightjar, albeit as a precusor to that societal setting. It is set in the same landscape, the Greensand Ridge, and about geographic and geological features that do exist, some of which might be found. Sandy, Stratford, Biggleswade and Beeston are all very real places, as are the quarry, iron age forts, owl, mouse, and number '6'. Whether you choose to find them, or not – the real and t' fiction – is entirely up to you, but what I do sincerely hope is you will enjoy this strange tale as much as I enjoyed the writing of it.

A quite eventful journey.

Yours,

Paul

* A list of all illustrations used is included at the end.

𝔗𝔢𝔪𝔭𝔢𝔰𝔱

Tempest
Chapter I Verse I

Quick, it happened, did seem, when it arrived, and yet for years the world did see and watch it come. Did nothing. Fed hate, sowed division, and ploughed fertile earth 'til dark seeds grew tall on thick stem. Black and strong, nettled, thorned, for good and bad, hate-filled flowers bloom. Beautiful they burst, bright to colour, fall as wildest storm, their petals pained. 'Tis fierce fury. Anvil-high clouds, as tower strong, let rain fall to dance heavy on the peoples of east and west. Tears of fell disgust. Lightening explodes, fills air electric. Crackles, hums, does let loose such angered hiss and light as kills. Thunder rolls, keeps time, rumbles low and drowns out the screams of death. A howling wind lifts waves from off the sea. Salted water to wash away all poverty and hope, the loves and life of souls despaired, their dreams discarded.

Lost.

Worthless.

Bodies carried out to sea.

The Tempest cleanses this world of sickness, of distilled promise, and brings with it cruelest change. See it play dark on the far horizon, taunts and toys with those as watch, wait, helpless spectators at their own demise. These are the people of the Commons; you and me, they, them, he, she, and it; and with them, so far apart, the Monsters cruel and the Respectable as worship them. From the simplest of men to the most noble of cruel, all do watch the Last Celebration begin. It is a storm, the Tempest, only today they call it *'t' Death'*.

Tempest
Chapter I Verse II

From ivory towers Monsters watch a coming storm. They see it far away. Peer ugly through gilded spyglass, decorated delicate in an ivy filigree. Eyes cold, hungry, huge they salivate. Drool sick anticipation, o'er bellys as bulge 'bout silken waistband. Theirs' is a greed as feeds a lean and barren soul. Blood pools dark in unbeating hearts, for it is they as birthed this storm, they...

Monsters.

As build it. Feed it. Gamble with the souls of others for the count of a pretty penny. A wealth untold they possess. Obscene. Diamonds glint and rubies glow red, coins of silver and gold weigh down heavy sacks; bottled black is the oil as spews deep from out the ground, and it is all theirs. It belongs to them. To...

Monsters.

As use silvered spoon to eat of bread and honey.

This is their world.

They own it.

Own it!

All of it.

Land and sea, countries, flags as flutter pretty in the wind, they own it all. The mountains tall, valley high, trees as dig deep the root, stone as holds up the tree, the gorge as cuts the land. They own it. City and town, small village, tiny hamlet, it all belongs to them. By hook and by crook they stole it, killed for it, earned it with all their ill-gotten gains. An old factory, brickbuilt chimneys tall that cough out black air and poison fields of green and gold as surround it; the crops as whisper soft in t' breeze, pretty ripples of wheat and rye, poppy, yellow rape. It's all theirs. The woodland, the rolling hills, chalk downs, and sandy beach, a pebbled way. It's theirs. They own it. The wildlife, road and rail, the planes on high as paint white lines in a sky of blue; the rivers and lakes, wide seas and all the fish as swim their way, trout, mackerel, herring an' more, they own it all.

Even rain in t' clouds, the colours of a rainbow and stars as twinkle bright. Or so they say. Rob of it. Steal of it. Plunder thoughtless and laugh at the money made. Fuel theft with a quiet despair and hidden hate of others. Those of the Commons.

Lesser folk.

The you and me, he, and she, they, them, those, and it, for they are the great unwashed.

Fools...

All of them.

There to be used and taken advantage of, kept in check by playing on a fear of anything different. A fear of folk not quite the same, not quite like them, for they will take what you now have. All others are a threat, especially any as is different; be it colour of skin or slant of eye, the cut of cloth or place of birth, creed, wealth, status, the Monsters will use it to keep themselves safe, for fear, it is a powerful tool. Cruel they play upon a fear of owning nothing, of being no one; of living in misery and poverty, destitute and abandoned forever, hated, disliked. Ugly. Fears the Commons do feel inside, cultivated loving, tended to careful by Monsters. You and me, he, she, it and they, all do feel such fear. And so, it is Monsters gamble on an outcome rigged. Make ever the more from out the people. Take ever the more from out the land. They own it all. Gaia screams.

Loud.

Dies slow her death. Plants wither. Animals starve. People die. But the Monsters care not. They make money, gold and silver, stock, and share. Own everything. Peer greedy on from towers tall and feed ever more a distant storm. Fill it with hate. Despair. Poverty and pain. With fear and greed, they poison the soil, strangle the air, and think idle to control that distant Tempest. Bathe happy in drips of honey, bread the flesh of others, and with silvered spoons do Monsters eat.

Tempest
Chapter I Verse III

There is no right,
There is no wrong,
But only for the good of me.

Was preached.

Nay.

Say not preached. Shouted from rooftops into households all o'er the land. From here to there, an' there to here, a sung message beamed unending. Mannequins dress pretty in suits of grey, dress of blue, neat cuts of finest cloth and fancied hair. Coiffured pretty, trimmed up delicate. Clever words are spoke from a silken mouth, bought tongue in cheek, and all of it respectable. For that is who they are.

The Respectable.

Voices trained. Mannerisms learned. It is they as are the warm and welcoming face of an autocue, paid pretty to be neutral. Paid pretty ne'er to think too deep and rewarded with celebrity, with wealth and a raised pedestal. Some are lifted up from out the gutter, trained as rats might be trained. Others are born with a silvered spoon. All are clever, in their way, and all of them do whisper soft, unthinking:

"...there is no right, there is no wrong,
but only for the good of me."

Come to believe it.

Why wouldn't they? Paid handsome not to think and sell happy the souls of others. Lose themselves to the message and become an advert for the words they read, the Monsters they serve. Made rich, rewarded greedy, they are trained as rats to forget the gutter and pass on silvered spoons to those of their own seed. Believe.

'Tis only for the good of me...

Tempest
Chapter I Verse IV

Sing…

'Tis only for the good of me,
The good of me,
The good of me;
'Tis only for the good of me,
That I am on this world.

The rest are taught. Common folk. You and me, they, them, he she, it and more sing the words aloud, in choirs. A hymn as reaches rafters high. Voices grouped by colours and creed, politics, sex, sin and more. Wrapped up in invisible chains, they sing of freedom. Dream of better lives. Lives forever out of reach, and as molluscs on the shore they are defined. Filtered food as sings in pretty colours, wonderful shapes, beautiful and ugly, and all do feed from off that message taught. They know no better. Sing songs of Monsters and, as if by magic, sleight of hand, they are taught to believe in a message pressed unseen upon them. Sold by preachers – the Respectable – dressed in suits of grey and dress of blue, hair coiffured, trimmed, cut pretty, sell the message crafted by Monsters in ivory towers that they too might become…

Rich!

And as a spell it is. Binded by hate and fear. Clever stitches sewn. Messages mixed and brewed, careful-made, and beamed into houses. From rooftops are the Commons taught to hate and fear. You and me, they, them, he, she, it, and more, are taught to despise and hate, to fear any as might want what is theirs. In choirs they sing, the same but not. Sing the same words to the same tune. He, she, they, them, it and more, you and me, beyond the sound of our own voices, own chorus, our own choir, we are deaf. And there does lie the enemy.

You and me.

He.

She.

They, them, it and more. All do want what I do have; would be who I am now. Would take it from me; steal of it, rob and leave me bloody, bruised upon the floor. Laugh at my distress, laud their triumph, and I fear them. They fear me. We come to fear anyone not quite the same, anyone who does not have what I have. Sing it loud.

'Tis only for the good of me,

The good of me,

The good of me;

'Tis only for the good of me,

That I am on this world.

And in ivory towers the Monsters tap baton.

Conduct.

From off the sea a Tempest rolls. Closer. Ever closer, until of a sudden it is upon them unexpected, yet not. There is naught anyone might do. Not Monsters in ivory towers. Nor the Respectable in their studios, and certainly not the Commons as are played, for they are all a part of it.

The Tempest.

Watch helpless on, unable to divert the wrath as rains violent down upon the world. In choirs they sing. Sing loud as ships go down about them. City and town, village, field, hill, sink beneath the ragged waves it brings, and there is no wealth of bread or honey as might save them now. All they might do is watch. You and me, he, she, they, them, it and more. The Monsters, their Respectable, the Commons, all drown in the storm that comes. Bodies float, flayed by wind, faces burned cruel in fires unchecked. But first does come the black blood coughed. Pestilence. Plague. A rider rich, as rides white horse, does gallop into view; with bow in hand does welcome in the end. Brings with him the first drops of rain on t' violent breeze, a sickness in the air.

Pestilence

Pestilence
Chapter II Verse I

Maggot remembers.

Just.

A child. Little more than a babe when Death does come a-dancing o'er the green fields of England. A sickness unseen, invisible, silent, unheard it creeps nasty from house to house, street to street. Enters by door o'er threshold, 'neath sill of window, and spreads from one room to t' next. In town and city, village, hamlet, the same; there is naught as might stop it. Not sky above nor mountain high, deep sea nor river wide. It travels happy with people and infects the world. There is no country safe, no land immune, no wall as might keep it out, and then, once inside, it does kill discriminate. Weak first, the old and sick, slow they drown in juices, cough up blood. Maggot remembers it vague. An ugly sound. Sickly perfume. Strange stills in a flickering film, the scenes mixed up and muddled. Dark memories of a mind that would heal itself.

Forget.

Only Maggot don't want to forget.
Not all of it.

Not Ma.

Sits by a bed and holds tight to her hand. Cold, it is. Plays idle with fingers blue and remembers a butterfly pretty in a meadow. Sees it fly funny. Flutters a flame o'er long grass and hears Ma laugh happy; does land her finger. Dances delicate there. She shows him. Hugs him close with her other arm. Warm. Beautiful. Wide wings fan themself slow. Open. Close. Open. Reds and orange, bright black and darkest white, the colours alive, on fire. She might be the most beautiful thing a child has ever seen. The butterfly.

A painted lady...

She calls it.

Ma.

Remembers her finger.

Blue...

And dead. Sometimes he thinks he sees her face. A glimpse. A pretty flicker. But he only ever sees the pretty; can't really remember what she looks like. Not properly. Not anymore. Pretty melts slow, as wax, and Pa cries quiet beside him. Sobs. Maggot kisses soft his cheek. Wet tears taste warm, bitter on whiskers short as bite, and Maggot tries then to see Pa's face too. Already it fades. Smells him warm, broad shoulders safe, forever strong; Ma's finger, cold an' blue, a butterfly bright. A painted lady pretty on the bedsheets bloody. Daisies dance, buttercups swoon, and Maggot feels grass play long 'bout skin of legs. Hears forever the laughter, loud and happy. Ma and Pa. Man, woman, husband, and wife. Lovers. Hears too a child, little more than a babe, and wonders if it's true. Listens the closer, and is lifted high by broad shoulders, strong arms. Cannot see their faces.

Does try.

Sees only a butterfly.

Pestilence
Chapter II Verse II

Pretty.

She rolls, the painted lady.

Rises.

Flutters funny.

Slow.

Maggot watches. Lies back against the bole of a tree, its thick roots twisted dark about him. Watches it climb air to where gilded leaf does hide the sky. It flies, a fashion of its own making – the butterfly. This way and that. Up. Down. Floats swell of a breeze and falls to laughter in a mind gone mad. Ma. Pa. His own. Watches, with exhausted eyes, a butterfly get to where it will. Sees it land the pink of foxglove, hears it ring a tiny bell. The butterfly warns Fae of monsters. Warns them of a Child of Man.

Man!

It is as kills the world. Man is monstrous; Maggot knows. Did bear witness to their crimes. So many crimes. Too many to count, to name, but first did come a sickness like no other. From East to West, it rides the sky, gallops o'er horizon to kill the old and weak first, the infirm. Cruel they drown in lungs. A killer. People hide. Lock themself away. Streets empty, and Pa is fearful; Ma does cry. Maggot plays the floor and listens to them talk. A sickness made by Man, some say on telly; others argue it is nature's way; but most do call it God's own curse, a vengeance on their evil. Pa don't know which is true. Maggot don't know either. Knows only that it came for Ma. Quick it takes her, and slow she dies. Healthy, worried one moment, a life worth living, sick and choking the next, a death prolonged.

And then she is dead.

Like that.

Just…

Gone.

Maggot remembers it vague. Pa sits helpless, watches sorry on, and he, the child, plays floor beside the bed. Hears her cough ugly. Harsh. It grates as nails in throat and chokes. Faint, Ma moans, weeps herself tired and knows she drowns in blood, in the mucus dark and thick as fills her lungs. Maggot recalls the towels, her bed, white sheets turned to red, bloody, sees wings of a butterfly. Water steams in bowls and Maggot plays the floor. Hears her die. A last gasp as takes forever.

Ma.

Is gone. And the wind sighs in trees.

Whispers...

Builds.

A voice.

Sunlight darkens. Wooded shadows gather, green, gold, black and dark, each as holds the other close. Might become something real as leaf ripples on high and branch creak. Maggot hears them groan, snap. Shadows spin wild, dance with the wind, lift fallen leaf, dark earth in hand. Twigs spin, swirl and twirl a frenzy, colours mix; green and gold of leaf and lichen, the black of earth and petal of fallen flowers become as delicate strokes of a painting. Slivers of reds and blue, pink, white, the Tyrian hues; a lost palette of woodland colour as swirls and twirls and spins the faster 'bout green darkness; sings song of sorts and does coalesce, slow becomes...

Beautiful.

Wind falls away. Sun shines bright, and from out wooded shadows a figure steps tall. Pale of skin, dark of hair, green eyes bright stars in night sky. Weak does Maggot smile, looks up and sees the worry in her face. He whispers soft, barely heard, and hopeful:

"Lady..."

And on her shoulder, the butterfly lands.

The Pity

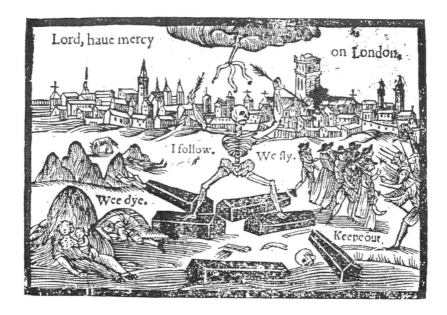

The Pity
Chapter III Verse I

There is no pity for the Dead, not in the numbers as die diseased, but it is the Dead as hold the world to account. Silent they scream, point, call out injustice and sing of all that is wrong. In waves they die. Each wave breaks bigger than t' next, and in piles, by pit, open graves, survivors drag the bodies. One corpse is thrown atop the next and cold are huge pyres raised; lit only when the stench is too much. Oldest die first, a span of years cut short at end, followed by the weak and sickly. Flames flicker too brief in memory of loved ones. And so it is until the fuel runs short and t' dead are left to rot out in t' open.

Miasma fouls the air, the living do fear the dead, and, still hungry, a contagion throws arms out wide, welcomes any as might come its way. Folk as cannot run, hide, escape, and in t' main it is poor as are taken, the Commons kissed. Ignorant of gender, creed, politics, race and role, the sickness takes numbers untold. Too many to count. They line the corridors of hospitals, sit floor, overwhelm doctors and nurses as fight for them; erode their number. Other trades die too. Those as keep clocks ticking. In city and town, village, hamlet, by nook and by crook, they die. All o'er the world the invisible needed are taken. Die. Cleaners, the builders of men, those as work road and rail, serve food, stock shelf. In classroom and factory they die, line furrows of field and litter the land. Scream silent and…

Point.

To ivory towers where Monsters watch, see; hear the scream and eat of bread, drip honey. In city mansion, grand estate, they huddle down to hide. Will weather storm and pray such pestilence does pass them by. It might take only the Commons. Some do die, Monsters, rich matyrs made, but for the most part 'tis only a scent of death tasted; the acrid smoke of burning pyres on tip o' tongue. But with that taste they begin to worry; feel then the Pity, for who will keep them, serve them, if not the Commons?

The Pity
Chapter III Verse II

It twists at Monsters' gut.

The Pity!

Haunts dreams.

Cruel shadows on a peaceful sleep, for who, if not the Commons, will pay them rent? Who will buy the goods, the services, they own? But it's worse than that and more. A realisation that it's the Commons, the poor, the unwashed and lowly as keep them in a manner to which they are accustomed. It is they, the Commons, the poor, as cut tree and break rock. They, the poor and the masses, as plunder land and sea for Monsters, pay then their taxes for the pleasure. 'Tis ugly and poor as do all the work. Stoke furnace, mine coal, sit line in factory and harvest fields, pick fruit, veg, butcher lamb. Place goods on shelf. It is the poor as pay the rich to eat, fly in t' sky, fish of sea. The Commons as dream of escaping gutter; will pay blood to achieve such wish. It is they, the downtrod, as make Monsters rich.

Rich.

And even as the Dead scream, point accusing, and Pity does twist cruel at gut, it seems the world herself does turn against the Monsters.

Mother Earth...

Begins to die.

Robbed of life, a plundered value, she can take no more. Land turns barren, goodness sucked from out veins; green fields turn to desert and forests burn. Huge fires, size of countries, roar red, char black; grey clouds and fine ash join hands with the black smoke of man-made pyres, fill the air and clog lungs. Rains flood, rivers drown, life itself does disappear. Animal, plant, birds in t' sky and insects on wing do die. Bees no longer buzz. Species fall extinct, even as the ice melts to reveal pus-filled wounds beneath. And in all the world, in all the lands, in all the peoples, 'tis Children of the Commons who see the harm that is done.

Children...

Who unite, lament, and join arms together. As one they sing, ignore unwritten rules of border and role, of creed and race, politics and more. It is children who break the rules of Monsters. Stand at last together, sing together. Songs of their own making. Beautiful songs. Songs that unite and bring folk together. It is children who join voice to sing of love and compassion, hope, justice, equality and change, such cruel sentiment as strikes fear into the hearts of Monsters, and it is then the unexpected happens; across generations, across borders of politics and creed, race, country, role, the Commons do heed the call of Children. Together they unite. Together as one.

Bang drum, blow trumpet, add voice and...

Sing.

Of freedom.

The Pity
Chapter III Verse III

Monsters hear them.

How could they not?

So loud, so sweet are t' voices of children. In white towers tall they listen and worry. Fret. Hear them sing. Worse. Hear adults join in and prefer instead the wails of woe, the screams of fear and hate to t' scent of hope that is on the air. A terrible perfume, pretty, and carried all o'er the world by winds whipped up in a storm of their own making. The Tempest howls loud about ivory towers, and in the drum of driving rain, to t' flash of lightening and roll of thunder, they hear the call for freedom. Monsters hear the Commons sing of hope, of equality and justice; do squirm uncomfortable. They are betrayed; by Gaia as dies, the Dead as scream and point, and now the Children who sing.

Unite

The Commons, the world, against them. Something must be done. A new song is needed. One as sows hate, breeds division. A song as kills all calls to freedom, to equality and justice. Words to set aflame the fear inside the Commons, to ignite their hate for others. Monsters call to them the Respectable; seek out wordsmiths as might oil wheels of propaganda; men and women who might strike a tune, play piano, compose a song to beam into the homes of all. Sing:

Hate them,
Fear them,
For they will take what you now have!

Hate them,
Fear them,
For they will kill you and then laugh!

Sing it loud.

A chorus of the Respectable beam it unending into houses and front rooms. Floral armchairs. Pretty faces in pretty suits, silk tie, and fancy frock tell any as will listen as to how *'They'* must be feared - *'the others'* – who will take all you now have, want all you now have. It is *'They'* who are all that is wrong with the world. Over and o'er, they repeat it, sing it, a mantra steeped in poison, soaked in lies. Twisted words as breed hate and promise aggression, violence. See poisonous souls lifted by the words, weak souls poisoned and lost, dragged down into the undertow by such ugly message. They are souls as do not see the Monsters as sit invisible on shoulders, wave baton and have them sing:

Hate them,
Fear them,
For they will kill you and then laugh!

A lie believed by many of the Commons.

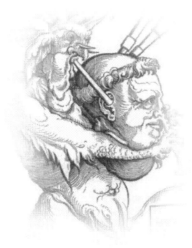

Too many.

The Pity
Chapter III Verse IV

Songs clash.

Loud.

Choirs take to streets.

Sing.

Be it for freedom or the status quo, good or bad, hate or hope, the voices rise and fall. Sing. And as waves they crash and break, foam, roar. Only now the Commons are not so easily deceived. Most do sing with the Children, see the Monsters for what they really are; selfish and greedy, hateful, cruel, and corrupt. With eyes wide open, they see instead the duplicity and fraud, the fostered hate and ignoble lie that Monsters seed and sow; will ne'er be played for Fools again. Together they take to the streets. Hear them sing of...

Hope.

And those as fear such change take angry to the streets; support the ways of Monsters and join voices to those of the Respectable. Sing loud and point hateful – *'For they will kill you and then laugh!'* – and believe it true. Loud their voices sing. Shout. Stand defiant and ugly; will not be moved as all about the Tempest blows wild. Wind and rain, the flash of lightning, roll of thunder, a call of drum.

Trumpets.

Sound.

A call to arms. Violence erupts. Sudden and sharp. Fuelled by hate and newfound love. For want of more, fear of less, the Commons and Monsters, the Respectable, take up arms, choose sides. In city, town, village, hamlet, field and furrow they sing, hold high their pitchfork and spear, a sword, gun, bow, blade. March to glory. Only then does the second horseman take to sky, gallops warhorse red to join a brother white. Armed and armoured, sword in hand and with lust for blood, it is War as stamps hoof and shakes world.

War

War
Chapter IV Verse I

Was cold when Pa did flee city. Dark. Lifts Maggot from out warm bed and carries him to car. A time near beyond memory. In t' darkness he hushes Maggot to quiet, opens car door and places him in the back, thows a blanket over his son's legs. "What's 'appening?"

"We're leavin'."

"Leaving?"

"Uh-huh." Pa nods, straightens blanket.

"Why?"

"It'll be safer."

"Safer?"

"Uh-huh."

"Where's safer?"

"Up north," Pa smiles soft, reassures, ruffles son's hair, "...place called Sotland." Maggot nods, sucks thumb, too sleepy yet to care. Pa closes the door. Lady from Upstairs already sits the front, looks back at him o'er her shoulder. Smiles. Maggot smiles back sleepy. Curls legs up underneath and sits knees. Presses his nose to the window. It's cold, the glass, icy 'gainst skin, and drops of water fall slow from top to bottom. Dance. This way, then that. Maggot follows them with eyes and finger. Feels car rock ragged as Pa climbs in behind steering wheel and closes the door; smiles at Lady from Upstairs. "You ready?"

She nods quiet. Smiles.

Says nothing.

Pa nods.

Keys rattle and engine starts.

Drops fall.

Trickle.

Slow they pull away.

Pa don't use the lights, and down dark streets they drive. A winding route by brooding hulks of terraced house and chimneyed stack. Cars litter road. Burnt out. Black shells. But a way enough is kept clear for small trucks to get through. This way that, Pa takes them in t' dark, by house and home, church and steeple; avoids the lights as flicker warm in t' distance, show where guards do man the barricades. On through night they drive. Follow darkness. By huge factory and bombed-out units, abandoned house and empty shop, Pa does take them ever north. Sometimes, inside buildings, fires flicker; show where people still eke out existence, a life. By their light Maggot sees graffiti blur, glimpses of bright colour and strange words in a dark world. Sees too the first silhouette of an angel as flies.

A woman...

Dark she swings.

Gentle.

From rope about her neck.

"You're sure this way's safe?" the Lady from Upstairs does ask. Pa nods, says nothing. They drive beneath the angel. Follow darkness. More frequent they fly – the angels – and slow they roll beneath them. By them. From lampost and tree, signs, they swing. So many. Forever on the rise, taking off. Maggot closes one eye – this one, then that – makes droplets run down o'er bodies and legs, arms; would see them drip from feet and hands. A game of sorts, one only a child is aware of. A challenge. If droplets drip from hands and feet, they will be safe.

From what?

Maggot don't know; knows only it's important.

War
Chapter IV Verse II

A city passes them by.

London...

Dark buildings, lost angels. Men and women, boys, girls, babes as sleep; others beaten bloody with bones as peek. Rats scurry, fox does scream and the car grumbles low beneath them. An age they drive, it seems, crawl in the dark and keep fires at bay. Maggot sits quiet in the back. Plays a game in his own little world and feels the car turn this way, that, until of a sudden they rise, climb.

Take off:

Fly...

O'er chimney and roof.

Fly...

Even now Maggot sees the look of a man they pass, pass level with his face. Angel dead, face bloated, bloody, beaten black and blue, he swings silent from a traffic light on the road below. One eye is closed shut, tight and blind, but his other stares at Maggot in a wide surprise; bids him fond farewell as the city falls away beneath them. An angel's look of disbelief is replaced by a thousand fires as flicker bright, stretch far away to the horizon. Candles as paint the sky an orange hue, a liminal glow, dark about the edge. Makes silhouettes of dark towers, buildings tall, pitch of roof and fall of chimney, the shadows of life, and still on they climb.

Weave this way, that, follow narrow gaps through burnt out car and hulk of lorry onto a bridge as crosses River wide. Still waters shimmer far below, turned silver in moonlight, and the dark backs of sandbanks break the surface as giant sea monsters on the move. On t' bridge they leave behind London. Bid farewell to house and factory, narrow lanes and dark roads, the guarded barricades, and flights of Angels. Descend the other side into a world of open fields and dark forest.

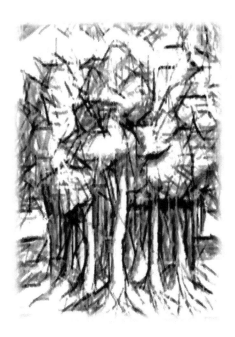

The sky is dark, stars bright, a three-laned road wide with a surface littered messy; the debris of those already fled, of those as have tried and failed. Lost lives in suitcases scattered. Clothes limp, dead bodies on t' floor. Pa does laugh relief at last, turns car lights on, and the Lady from Upstairs does lean across the seats to hug him tight. "We's made it!" laughs happy, does kiss Pa's cheek. "Aye," Pa grins back, nods, laughs quiet, "...we're safe."

Safe.

Maggot smiles inside. Enjoys happy in the front seats and follows a droplet of water on the outside of his window. It twists cunning, clever, dances strange and would trick him shrewd, but Maggot moves his head and closes a practiced eye. Follows it careful down t' glass, makes it drip into the mouth of a corpse. One as sits blackened, twisted on side o' road. Licks then the window and tastes it cold.

Safe.

On a road as takes them north.

War
Chapter IV Verse III

"RUN!"

Safe...

Pa did say. Only 't isn't.
"RUN!"
And Maggot runs.

Uphill.

Steep. The Lady from Upstairs does pull his arm, drags him up that slope as fast she might. By tree, through leaf, they hurry. 'Tis autumn, and gilded leaf does lie a crunched-up carpet, thick 'neath foot, gold-green on t' boughs above. High in the sky the sun is bright, cold, far away, and all about their breath does cloud a mist. People shout angry behind them. Harsh. Strangers as run loud. Snap branch, stamp leaf, fly a flag o' Monsters, white lightening on blue sky, a field of blood. Maggot can't see them, but loud they echo in t' trees.

On they run.

Hurry.

Hill steep beneath them.

"Quick!" the Lady from upstairs does hiss, pulls an arm and drags Maggot small up a sheer bank. Stops a moment, a pause in her run to push him up ahead of her. "Now go," she hisses breathless, "...quick!" And on Maggot runs. Through leaf and cold air, by trees as watch, and behind him she follows. Slips. Stands and looks back o'er a shoulder, her knees wet. But a moment before she follows at a run, catches him up again and takes his hand. "This way," she gasps. Together they run. Follow now a narrow holloway as circles the summit of a hill. Trees crowd close about. Watch on. Giants of girth and huge of root. Ancient creatures as look sad upon them. Old oak, chestnut, giant elm, and wizened yew, silver birch; all do see the fear as takes them. And it had all been going so well...

War
Chapter IV Verse IV

Come dawn, the cold sun rises bright and Lady from Upstairs does open a tin. Breaks cake. Pa drives north. Ever north. The cake is nice. Maggot picks at currents, nibbles a mouse. Light crumbs litter his top and the seat he sits. Idle he brushes at them, sits quiet and listens to grown-ups talk. It's the Old North Road they take – Pa says – Ermine Street as once was called; leads all the way to Scotland, Edinburgh, and is better than using a motorway. "Why?" the Lady from Upstairs does ask.

"Safer."

Lady eats cake.

Pa sniffs, nods as his want when wise, "Less as like t' be watched."

Lady nods.

Eats.

Maggot sits knees, pushes his nose to the cold window. A flat land blurs by, reflects, the going quicker now that day is on them. Green fields, low tree-topped hills, the sight of Man every now and then. The edge of a town in t' distance, a farm or village surrounded by field and furrow, abandoned petrol stations, and grey industrial estates as hug ground; old units and factories that try to hide in the landscape. Some still sit whole, others no more than rubble and ruin. In places, smoke rises where pockets of life still live, hide, survive, and cars litter the side of the road. Abandoned, forgot, burnt black. In places, Maggot sees packs of men and women, boys, girls, folk too old to move proper, digging hungry at dirt in t' fields. Some bodies don't move; lie still, sit funny, limbs all twisted strange and awkward. Slow they drive them by, the living and the dead. Haunted eyes as follow, watch them, cold, and then does come the tunnel. Pa it is as says to look out the front window, calls out to Maggot and nods his chin.

Huge!

It is.

The tunnel...

Giant mouths as gape. Huge they are, wide open in a hill of glass and stone. One this side of the road, and one the other. Black maws of hungered dark. Maggot stares wide-eyed, moves quick to the gap in t' front seats, the better to see. Leans forward eager 'twixt Pa and t' Lady from Upstairs. Might be to enter is to disappear forever, to find there a world unknown. Surely a place of dragons and wyrm. Closer they come, crawl forward, and Maggot cranes his neck to better see. Mouth dark, wide, tall before them, does wonder how the weight of the world does balance the back of a tunnel.

Pa brakes.

Gentle.

Stops.

A moment...

Quiet they sit. A lorry lies its side, trailer and spilt load strewn across three lanes; makes it impossible to see what lies beyond; to see the road inside t' tunnel. "Is it safe?" the Lady from Upstairs whispers. "Don't know," Pa answers truthful, sniffs, looks to her worried beside him. Helpless shrugs, "...but we 'as t' try."

The Lady nods. Smiles. Touches Pa's hand gentle, "I know."

Pa sighs deep.

Decides.

Nods.

Looks to Maggot as leans the gap between them "Is it exciting?"

Maggot nods.

Smiles.

"Are there dragons?"

"Dragons?"

"Inside?"

Pa laughs a smile, touches Maggot's cheek affectionate and strokes it gentle, "Shall we see?"

Maggot nods.

Come on then," Pa breathes deep, drops hand to steering wheel and grips it tight, knuckles white, "...let's see what's inside." Lady from Upstairs does nod, breathes deep and holds breath as Maggot leans excited between them. Slow does Pa move the car forward.

Cautious.

Rounds lorry and takes them in.

Concrete looms heavy above, overhead, might bite, fall, a toothless maw as stretches wide, and darkness enfolds them quick. Pa turns the lights back on. Cars litter the Underworld. Abandoned lorries, vans, a strange graveyard. Shells all burnt out, black and cold the metal bones. Maggot follows the dark shadow above as eats light. Leaves the gap in the front seats to kneel on the seat and watch it eat from out the back window. The mouth of the tunnel shrinks ever smaller behind them, tiny, 'til at last it disappears. Only then does darkness rule complete. Maggot returns to the gap in the front seats, watches Pa weave slow in the darkness. Careful. Headlights stopped from ever penetrating far by the metal bones and broken hulks. Motes of dust ficker and take flight in t' beams, dance, and the last gasps of smoke from fires turned cold swirl faint and ghostly.

At the halfway point, deep in t' darkness, they come to a barricade broken. Lost banners, tired flags, flutter limp in a world of no wind, and dead men stare. Blind eyes as look in through the windows. Lost souls all killed in a fight forgot. But there are none there alive as try to stop them. On Pa drives. Picks a way through debris and dirt until, at last, they see the other side.

Daylight...

Bright.

In t' distance.

Hope.

Maggot laughs happy, points, and Lady from Upstairs does breathe deep a sigh of relief. Maggot wonders if she has held her breath the whole way. Even Pa relaxes, grins. A smile that grows ever the wider, like the light that pulls them on. A beacon of hope. Ever closer, wider, until the light laps gentle at the darkness, ripples barely felt, and then, of a sudden and without warning, it is that they are out the other side. Blink blind in brightness. Maggot frowns disappointed, rubs eyes, "No dragons!" and the Lady laughs. Pa does pull his son into a one-armed hug, whispers a loving kiss, "No dragons," laughs, "...but we're safe now."

Safe.

Now.

Only Pa is wrong.

Violence

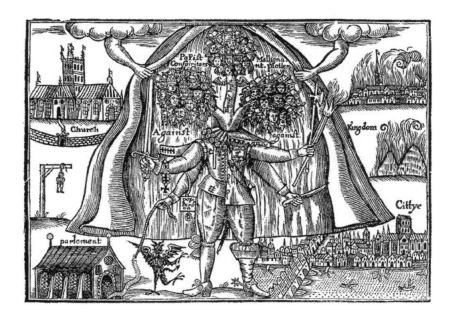

A Nonsense Rhyme

THREE headless men do play at ball;
A handless man, he serves them all;
Mouthless men do stand and laugh,
And legless drags his cloak.

Original discovered in a manuscript of 1480;
Held in the Bodleian Library, Oxford.

Violence
Chapter V Verse I

Flags are raised on high for all to see.

Old flags.

New.

Pretty!

A world divided by the flutter of colours, united in hate and fear of each other. Some want to see the world change for the better, fight for equality, justice, rights of the Common Man. Others believe the world ought stay the same, be as it has always been, and they do fight for the status quo, the right to enrich oneself. Each does see t' other as wrong.

Evil.

And believe it.

Families are torn apart, the heart of nations and city, colour, creed, race, split asunder, not by sword but by belief. From out the depths of the Commons new leaders rise, generals and saints, false prophet, and lowly queen. In city and town, market square and village street, they preach, call out from the pulpit, sing. People listen. Join in with them and believe. Cry out for justice, for equality, hope, raise new banners pretty. Gather. March. Monsters scream defiance. See new the colours and raise high the flags of old. It is a call to arms.

WAR!

Inevitable.

Tears world apart.

Violence reigns supreme and naught is sacred. Not church or chapel, steeple, the altar, priest, or nun. Towns and city burn divided, kingdoms and country a cesspit of hate. It is a world on fire, aflame, hatred is spread by voice, by the bleeding of others. Men and women, young and old, flock to banners and choose sides. For love or hate they march and sing united, each to face the other. There are no borders, no rules, and bright do weapons glint. Catch light of moon and star, sun, the flicker of a torch, and red do gutters flow, as rivers run. By fen and field, alley, snicket, room, and road, they fight. Kill.

Children cry.

Die.

There are no prisoners taken, no captives made, no mercy. Such is the hate as infects them all. Gibbets are made, lamposts used, and the dance of death ensues. People jig at end o' rope, families taken, shot in lines and murdered; deep pits filled. Bones break surface, white and barren crop, then bodies left to lie. So it has always been in such times. In war. Violence breeds of violence, cruelty as a game, a sickness from out a never-ending cup as infects soul unseen. None are safe. Men and women, boy, girl, young, old, babes in arm, staked and crucified. Ever more horrifying the means, is pain inflicted, and louder the cheers as laugh. See, the celebration. There is no one safe. Not kings or queen, man, mother, child, and Monster. All do scream. Die.

𝕸𝖆𝖌𝖌𝖔𝖙

Maggot
Chapter VI Verse I

"Hurry!"

Maggot does. Looks over a shoulder and sees shadows in the trees. Voices shout. Dogs bark. Come closer. The Lady from Upstairs sobs, runs, pulls him on by leaf and branch, o'er root; looks back and sobs the more. Pulls him on. Brambles bite, tiny teeth, needles cruel as snag at clothes and rip thread, but she cares not. Maggot loses his scarf, one as Ma did knit. Red it falls from shoulders and lies a gilded floor. He looks to where it is and might run back to get it, but the Lady won't let him. She holds tight to his hand and hisses, "This way!"

Pulls him on and follows the holloway as leads uphill. Narrow it is and steep the hill does rise to t' left, all rock and tree, fern and frond. Falls equally steep away to t' right beneath them. Maggot looks to the canopy above. Gold and green of leaf, hint of fire, black branches blur, and, far above them a cold sky. It seems the way they follow leads to the summit. A trail made by a thousand feet o'er a thousand years; of deer and wolf, fox, bear, and painted men. On they run, follow the trail until it skirts an old oak as overhangs steep slope below.

Wide it is.

The tree...

Huge.

An age beyond the tell of years, twisted root as lift it up from out the ground and make it seem to walk. Leaf lies a golden blanket all about, thick drifts as roll in waves downslope, and therein the corpse of a fox. It stinks, some time dead. Worms writhe ugly, fall white from mouth and crawl from nose, do make it move. Maggot gags. Might be sick, the perfume so thick, but not the Lady from Upstairs.

She stops. Sees there...

Hope!

However small.

Maggot
Chapter VI Verse II

The car screams, wheels screech, rubber burns; "They're following us!" the Lady from Upstairs hisses sharp, looks over her shoulder by Maggot, who is thrown 'cross back seat. "I know," Pa growls checks rear-view mirror and takes them across the A1 in a sharp turn. Maggot clambers back to knees, looks out window. Behind them, where flags flutter bright and a tall barricade stands, four-wheel drives screech out onto road, followed by an old flatbed with mounted guns. Horns sound loud, give chase. Pa accelerates, uses gears and makes engine whine, leaves main road, and throws the car to the left; follows a country lane. The Lady from Upstairs still stares scared out the back window. "Can we get away?"

"We can try!" and by wooden pallets, stacked mountain high, they scream, across a narrow bridge o'er small river. Take-off wild o'er bumps in road. Still the people behind give chase, follow, but Pa gains distance on them. Wheels screech ugly about a bend where a large sign shouts 'TESCO'; beneath it the cold bones of a burnt-out store point heavenward. Maggot holds to the door. Watches cars and four wheels bounce wild o'er the bridge behind them. Flatbed brings up the rear.

Beeston...

That place is called. Pa reads name from off a sign where a mouse and owl sit and play; points them out to Maggot with a smile before the world comes back to haunt them. It's the Lady from Upstairs who sees the barricade first. Shouts. Points. Flags flutter from off a metal footbridge, white lightning strikes, and dead heads gaze down onto the road from crude spikes raised on high. People stand guard, heavy armed with lorrys and trailers set to block road. Only a narrow way is left about the bridge, where small cottages watch on pretty in pink and pastel blue; see a barren place of hate and metal, of violence, where Monsters wait with friends. Without thought Pa turns, flees, grinds car o'er central reservation in a cloud of dust; leaves the main road where mouse and owl still play.

Maggot
Chapter VI Verse III

Hurried does the Lady from Upstairs lift Maggot, steps down from off the path and places him careful 'neath the twisted roots of that old oak. Finds a dark nook of earth beyond where the dead fox lies and pushes gilded leaf from off the floor about him. "Hide here," she whispers, does hide that place from sight, "...and stay quiet."

Maggot nods, says nothing.

"Promise?"

"I promise."

"Good," she nods. Smiles.

"Where are you going?"

"Not far." The Lady brushes hair from out his eyes. "I just need to get those people away from you. Then I'll come back."

"You will?"

"Of course."

"And then we'll go get Pa?"

"Yes," the Lady sobs, "...then we'll go get Pa."

Maggot nods, reassured. Down the hill, in among trees and green shadows, people shout ugly, loud. She glances back o'er her shoulder, brief, kisses him quick, a feather-touch on his forehead. It's the first time she's kissed him, and she holds tight to his arms, brings his eyes to her, face serious. "Lie still, don't let no one see you," Maggot nods, "...and stay quiet as a mouse!"

Maggot would nod again, but she is already gone; disappears back up o'er root and earth. He sits quiet instead. Doesn't move but for a wrinkling of his nose at the heavy scent of dead fox and thick earth, damp leaf and rotting bark. Hears footsteps run above him. They come close. Heavy boots as stand level with the oak. A man it is as follows the path with dogs on a rope. An age it seems he stands there, breathing ragged from the run. One of the dog sniffs at the oak, but the handler sees only the dead fox and drags it angry away. Kicks it.

"THERE!" a man shouts loud from top o' hill, "THIS WAY!" Hounds bark and heavy boots hurry on. Climb up away from where Maggot peers through twisted roots. Sits quiet and listens to them run uphill. Wild barks and angry shouts as follow others and leave him be. Slow they fade to silence.

Disappear.

Still, he does not move.

Sits quiet.

Watches...

Worms wriggle in soil and flesh, crawl 'bout fox and fall from fur. Beetles too, grey, and black. Small they scurry, feast. Maggot sees so much life where death does dwell.

Sits still.

Hears...

Nothing.

Snuggles down in golden leaf, back to the bole of a tree; its twisted roots a roof above him, dark earth a wall about, he hugs knees to body and studies colours. Fungi pretty. Delicate. Brown, white, the brightest red. Old rot. Mossed bark. Yellow lichen and the glint of stone crystals in black soil. Rich earth. Fertile. Maggot shivers. Wonders when the Lady from Upstairs will come back.

Closes eyes. Falls asleep.

𝔄lone

Alone
Chapter VII Verse I

When Maggot wakes the sun is low, a ball of fire as sinks down in trees and makes of them the blackest silhouette. Monsters thin with shadows long, arms gnarled, hands cruel, twisted fingers as reach out to kill. Maggot shivers, begins to feel the cold and fright of a wood at night. Huddles down into the warmth of a coat and hugs knees to body, does wish he'd not dropped his scarf. Thinks perhaps to go and get it and peeps quiet through roots. Decides better of it and stays still. Stays where he is, and watches blind the sunset; sees red light bathe a world in fire.

Brief.

And then comes dusk. A grey darkness as creeps from shadows, leeches colour from out the world. Gold turns to blue, greens to grey and brown to black, every shade of cold in between. Maggot sniffs. Pulls armfuls of leaf close about him and piles it high, a blanket for warmth, a wall of sorts for protection. Finishes just as night descends, a darkness so complete it swallows everything. Blind, he is, Maggot. Might have been okay with that, but for the sounds. Ghosts, monsters of dreams and mare, crack branch, snap bark, and he hears an invisible tread of naught in leaf. Whimpers soft and, might cry; closes eyes to hide the better and listens blind.

Darkness laughs.

Cruel...

From somewhere out beyond the hole he sits. Wonders then where the Lady from Upstairs is? Pa? Wishes they were there with him. Lips move, child's prayer unanswered, and darkness creeps closer. Moves. Someone coughs, near to hand and Maggot hides head in arms, eyes tight shut, and whispers silent:

Go 'way!

Wishes it loud.

Please!

Does not see the eyes as watch. Low to the ground they are. Catch light of star, glint black o'er a mouth as chews leaf 'neath ugly tusk. Horns of the devil upon its head, it studies the child and wonders idle what a babe o' Man does in t' woods at night. Moves careful, quiet, silent in darkness, then pulls at a branch and cracks it loud. The boy whimpers and in response that beast does cough loud in warning. Another does come close to see. A pretty mate as fades to view from out the darkest shadows, peers from where bramble broils and sharp thorns snick. Sees the child and bears witness to strange event. They stay a moment, chew leaf, then wander off together, amble slow away by branch.

Muntjac.

Maggot cries. Scared. The night so loud. Hears scream and screech, snick and snuffle, cruel laugh, strange cackle; there's a hacking cough, and twigs and branch break loud 'neath a tread of giants. Leaf does whisper secrets, a rustle as ne'er does stop, and noses sniff in hungry huffle, do wonder what a babe does there. Hedgehog, rabbit, vole, and mouse. An invisible fox creeps close, sneaks, peeks, then runs. Others wander by. Red deer, badger, an owl as perches in the tree above, and bats as flit blind by branch. Even the trees do seem to move. Creak. Walk in t' night. Dark shades as might lift him up in cruel arms sharp and eat him whole. Maggot cries in the darkness, sobs soft, and does wish the Lady from Upstairs'd come back. Pa, from out the car. Would have them with him now and don't remember the sleep as creeps upon him soft; quiet it lifts him, to dreams filled with t' sounds of nightmare. Dogs bark, wheels scream, men shout wild and Pa bleeds. Red it drips, bright down his face. The Lady from Upstairs does pull Maggot from out the car, drags him off into the trees.

Run!

She shouts.

Run!

And Maggot does; he runs as fast he might.

Alone
Chapter VII Verse II

It is the first night of many. Maggot don't know how many, stays hid beneath the tree.

Three sleeps?

Six?

Maybe eight or ten, but it's difficult to know for a child as cannot count. He knows to three well enough, can sometimes count to five an' six, but by eight and seven and twelve it all gets muddled up. Does do as the Lady from Upstairs did tell him. Stays hid 'neath tree. Waits patient and gets hungry. Thirsty. Drinks water as drips from leaf and root. Opens mouth to catch it clever, or sups from where it gathers in an old crook of wood. Icy cold it is. And he eats berries black as hang helpful down from a bramble through gap above. Same berries he did once collect with Ma from off a hedge.

Eats them hungry.

Messy.

Sweet...

Juice as dribbles tasty down his chin. Licks fingers, sticky, but they aren't enough. Hunger bites, tummy rumbles. Hurts. Twists tight. He thinks to eat the flesh of fox. Looks, but decides better of it. Worms writhe, fur moves, and thick perfume he hardly smells still tells him not to. Looks elsewhere instead. To mushroom and fungi, blade of leaf and green of grass, the lichen as clings to trees. He nibbles it careful. Some, brown and fleshy, taste nutty and of the earth, and one as clings to tree does even taste of chicken. Others, thin of body and broad of cap, poke delicate through leaf and soil. They look as if they dance, dressed pretty in golden brown and earthenware, periwinkle hoods, and bodies white. The only ones he doesn't try are those as glisten red, like blood, drip black. Avoids those as Ma did once tell him ne'er to pick such mushrooms. Nibbles t' others careful, but mainly eats the berries. Picks by day, eats at dusk, and watches sunset before another night does come again. Dark. Black. A cloak upon the world.

Scary!

That first night. Next one too. But as time passes so too does fear. Young eyes become accustomed to the darkness, and Maggot begins to see the things as make the noise. Hides quiet in the piles of leaf he pulls in warm about and watches them. Sees hedgehog huff, tall on short legs, and badgers snuffle, grunt, churr, wail and waddle noisy through the leaf. Smiles at a pretty fox as eyes him wary from 'neath bramble, afeared o' dead brethren as lies the foot of tree. It laughs loud a warning to others, then quietly disappears; less than a shade it seems. Deer cough, owls scream, mice do skitter and dart, run. Rabbits come close enough to touch, hop lazy 'bout his feet, and ferrets shriek. Deer eat of tree, snap loud the branch, stamp at ground, then fade as ghosts before his eyes. Silent. Magic. Wondrous does he see the world anew. Fear leaves him. Sleep comes easy, but hunger will not go away. With every day, every dawn, at dusk and at night, he grows the weaker. Becomes too weak to walk.

To sit.

Too weak to pick of berry.
Lies still.
And…

Alone
Chapter VII Verse III

Maggot thinks he might die.

Sleep forever.

Looks to leaf against the sky. Dark and gold, green, orange, red and black the silhouettes. Listens to wind sigh. Branches creak far above, a whisper as builds.

Strange...

Turns to a whistle, and as if annoyed the sunlight darkens. Dances a ripple in leaf far above. There, where branches sway ominous, creak hypnotic. Maggot's eyes flutter, blink. Sees dark shadow gather close about the tree. It hugs at branches, curls about trunk, and touches the roots where Maggot hides. It is the shadow as calls the wind to dance.

Exhausted, tired, Maggot pushes himself up, leans back against the tree and sees wind swirl wild. Lifts leaf litter in arms and throws it crazed up into air. Small twigs and gilded leaf, acorn cup, green nettle, brambled thorns fly. It is a wild whistle as sings a tune, the sun a long way off and banished high. The faster it twirls and spins, the wind, a shadow, a tapestry of autumnal colour as dances green.

Pretty!

'Neath tree.

Sees a lady step from out its midst, does slow become beautiful, as of another world. Wind, leaf, drops quiet down about her, a woodland cloak as covers silvered gown of coldly frost. Pale, she smiles, soft, sad, green eyes the promise of springtime, hair as darkest night, and she stands so he might see her. Holds out a caring hand. Beckons him come. With the last of his strength, the last of his will, Maggot stands brittle. Legs wobble, world spins strange, and he staggers out from 'neath the oak as has been his home. Is lifted quick and quiet in gentle arm. "Hush now," she whispers soft against an ear, "you're safe now."

Peg

Peg
Chapter VIII Verse I

Maggot knows not how long he sleeps. A day, week, month, year, it matters not in the tell of time to some, and such it is with the lady as finds him. All Maggot knows is that when he does at last wake up, he's warm to t' bone; toasty, as he hasn't been for the longest time. A thick blanket, patches of woodland colours, covers him from chin to toe, and a small fire burns bright in the small hollow he finds himself in. It cackles happy. Spits sparks and bright embers as twist and twirl away into the darkness. Turn there to stars. It's night-time and he blinks sleepy, sees moon bright through leaf.

"Hello."

Eyes open wide.

In the darkness her voice is as a songbird unseen, sweet notes clear as dew, and it draws him to the far side of the fire; sees there the lady from a dream. Beautiful she sits, fair by night as she was in a sleeping mind. She smiles one sided at him, friendly, pup-pups clay pipe from the other side of her mouth. It lights her strange, from 'neath; a delicate chin, blue smoke as curls fragrant 'bout features, dances there brief, a soft swirl in the breeze before it disappears into dark of leaf and night above. Maggot frowns cautious.

Stranger danger...

Ma and Pa did teach him of it. People might be dangerous, even as they act friendly, and so he considers it careful. Thoughtful. It must be she as did find him weak beneath the tree, carried him here, wrapped him warm in a blanket and laid him out by the fire. Now she smiles friendly, smokes pipe (strange but equally interesting), and has kept him safe while he slept. Even so, for a young 'un, it's a troublesome decision when you've only just woken up. "Hello," Maggot whispers a frown. Pushes himself to sit and fixes blanket warm about legs. All the while she watches him, a wry smile on lips as might laugh, smokes patient, and waits as he studies her, takes in his surroundings.

Warm light flickers pretty. Dances merry about t' edge of a hollow and keeps night at bay. In the dark beyond trees circle, the forest close, branch and leaf as a sheltered roof above. Logs are placed about the fire, to sit on and keep flames controlled, and a large metal pot dangles from chains on a tripod. Whatever it holds bubbles happy, flames as lick bottom, and t' smell of food is delicious. Maggot breathes it deep. Sees then a hedgehog. It sits a prickly ball beside him, all but invisible on a log, and watches him funny; cocks head inquisitive, pointed nose atwitch and black eyes bright. Tests air. Sniffs him out. Maggot laughs surprised, happy at such a sight; begins then to notice other animals dotted about the hollow. A fox lies curled about the lady's feet, one eye open as it sleeps, and mice scuttle about the logs as rabbits peep wary from out beneath. In the shadows behind her, a golden doe moves cautious into the edge of light, eats shroom from off the floor. And all about her moth and butterfly flutter pretty. Leaf rustles soft, a whisper from above. Maggot lifts eyes; sees white ghost in branches. For the longest moment it sits unmoving. Then blinks.

An owl.

Beautiful.

And with the blink of a bird, a ghost, all fear, worry, does leave the child. It seems she, the lady, is as one of them. Wild and of the forest. Quiet she sits. Pup-pups pipe and smiles knowing at young eyes as look back to her then. Study her. "You must be hungry."

Maggot nods.

"Good." As a breeze she moves, stands pretty in silvered dress and autumnal cloak. A Princess of the Trees as ladels broth into a wooden bowl. It steams hot. One ladel. Two. Then three and four, and all the while she pup-pups her pipe; hands the filled bowl and wooden spoon to the boy as waits. "Thank you."

"You're welcome," she nods, blows a cloud of smoke, and retakes her seat opposite. Removes the pipe from her mouth, and points at the bowl he cradles warm in hand with its stem, "Now eat it all." Maggot nods earnest; will do as is told and spoons it hungry to mouth. Eats his fill, and all the while she watches quietly on.

Peg
Chapter VIII Verse II

Maggot licks the bowl clean, a taste of nut and earth, shroom and wild garlic warm inside. Sucks spoon. "Good," the lady smiles. Stands tall to take t' bowl and spoon from off him. Studies it empty, "...you'll feel the better for it."

"Thank you," Maggot nods, grins. Watches quiet on as she retakes her seat and places the bowl on t' floor beside her. Mice investigate. Run and hurry from off the logs, scurry and jump from out under leaf, and stand tall the hind legs. Tails long, nose atwitch, they sniff, squeak disappointed and run this way, that, one over t' other to check the far side of bowl and spoon. The pretty lady watches their antics, chuckles soft with a smile, and looks to the boy opposite, "You left them none."

"Oh," Maggot frowns, "I'm sorry."

"No," she laughs with a shake of her head, "youse does need that food far more 'n they'll ever do!" nods to where they still scurry-hurry, flitter 'bout feet with nose and tails atwitch. See there is none left and hop, climb, leap, and jump back onto logs. "Far too many tubby tums in 'mongst that lot."

Maggot laughs.

Lady smiles. Does make to load her pipe under his watchful eye. Long stemmed, white, it is. Made of bone, perhaps, and carved as a branch 'bout which leaf of ivy climbs. Where it widens at the bowl, leaf turns magic into Celtic sworls, becomes then the babes of Man as dance there intricate. Girls and boys. She taps the bowl clean on the log beside her, blows into it and looks. Nods satisfied. Pours dried leaf then from out a pouch on her belt into the palm of her hand. Gentle, she swirls the bowl in a soft spiral atop the leaf, sets children to dance about the bowl and, as if magic, the pipe does fill itself. Spies then his eyes watching and smiles soft at the wonder; finishes off with a loose topping of dry leaf and checks the draw unlit.

Pup-pup...

Nods satisfied at t' flow.

Smiles...

Maggot smiles back. Watches on as she leans forward and takes a brand from out the fire; lights the pipe with a couple of 'pup-pups' and then tamps down the leaf; does light it again. Blue smoke, a heady and fragrant perfume, billows a cloud about her, fills hollow, and Maggot lifts chin to watch it rise to dance with leaf and star, wrap 'bout branch, fore it disappears, invisible on t' air. Only after a second toke, a much longer, more considered...

Pup-pup!

Does the lady lift green eyes to study him; the child as sits opposite. "So," she says at last, a long moment of quiet 'fore she speaks; points at him with the stem of her pipe, "...tell me now your name." He sits tall then, upright, and proud as one ought when a name is exchanged, does tell the name as Ma did always call him affectionate. "Maggot."

Peg
Chapter VIII Verse III

"Maggot!" and t' lady's eyes do wide surprise. Brows arch on high and she holds the pipe open-mouthed, slim fingers 'bout stem and bowl. For a moment she forgets to smoke, studies him suspicious down a pretty nose and thinks he surely teases. Sniffs. "Maggot?"

"Yes."

"You're sure?"

"U-huh!" Maggot nods true, explains, "It's not my real name, just what everyone calls me."

"Everyone?"

"Everyone."

"Well," lady shakes her head one-sided, chuckles wry, "youse the first Maggot ... not of a wormkind ... as I's ever has met."

"Really?"

"Really!" she laughs, chews pipe. Smokes.

Pup-pup.

Narrows eyes thoughtful and breathes blue smoke out 'bout words, "Why does they call you Maggot then?"

"Why?"

She nods, "'Tain't common."

"Well," Maggot frowns serious, for all names, nicknames included, are a serious business, "Pa did say it was Ma called me it."

"Ma?"

"Uh-huh," Maggot nods. "She said I did look like a Maggot when I was born." The lady laughs. A proper laugh, like rain in trees, and Maggot smiles at the sound. Waits patient. In time she stops, grins and smiles friendly; "And where's Ma now then?"

"Now?"

She nods.

"Dead."

"Oh," lady's smile does disappear, "I'm sorry."

"Died o' sickness," Maggot explains, "some time since."

"And Pa?"

"He's 'ere," Maggot looks out about the hollow, "…somewhere."

"'Ere?"

"Yes. And the Lady from Upstairs."

"The lady from upstairs?"

"Uh-huh." Maggot frowns serious. "She was meant t' come back."

"Come back?"

"To get me."

"Get you?"

"Yes."

"But she didn't?"

"No."

"No…" the lady echoes thoughtful sad. Sits quiet. Chews pipe and pup-pups frown. Maggot watches the small hedgehog eat a worm. It's an earthworm. Long. Muddy and wriggly, and he decides (earthworm half-eaten) that now is the polite time; looks back to the lady with nose wrinkled serious and asks, "What's your name?"

"My name."

"Yes."

"Mmm…" She smiles wistful. Looks back in mind and remembers so many names from times long gone. Ages forgot to memory of most. Sees druids old, beards long, wrinkles deep and breasts fallen ugly. Wise and haggard, beautiful they are. Do worship her a Goddess. Do worship her brothers and sisters too. Women of the Ways, Men of the Wood, powerful and of the trees, of moon and star and sun, the earth underfoot and sky far above. Bow down low, lead blue-painted in song and dance 'bout tree and stone. So many names they are called. Witch, and daemon, angel, hag, warlock, nymph, Lady, Lord; virginal pure. They are cailleach, lost souls forgot, Children of the Mother, and they are Andraste and Angharad, Hag of Hair and Churnmilk Peg. Fflur to some, Freya to others. So many names echo in time, sound out across the years. Most forgot. Man does call them Hecate and Golleuddydd, Kerhanagh *'the Deville's Mother'*, Mórrígan *'the Queen'*, Alisansos, and the Green

Man. They are one and all. Sisters. Brothers. Kings and Queens, forever of the world and forever feared, loved, worshipped, remembered. A log falls in the fire, cracks loud, cackles and sends embers into stars. She remembers all her names and looks wry to Maggot. Quiet he sits.

Patient...

Waits.

"Peg," she smiles, nods. Pup-pups pipe and nods again, "Yes," she decides, grins broad, face pretty, "...you can call me Peg."

Peg
Chapter VIII Verse IV

"Peg," Maggot echoes. And so it is they are known to each other. Peg to Maggot, Maggot to Peg. They talk idle, a muchness of nothing. Wood cracks and snaps, cackles in the fire and listens; sends embers bright and high to dance in the dark. Maggot tells Peg of London, of a drive through the night and tunnels where dragons might still live. Peg listens quiet.

Patient.

Pup-pups...

Pipe.

And asks questions polite. Here and there as animals snuffle and snort, sniff, and explore the child as sits their midst. They have no fear of him. Not mouse nor rabbit, ferret, mole or the hedgehog as grumpy huffs, its tummy full of earthworm and wanting sleep. It seems they all live with Peg, in the hollow, and Maggot laughs happy, enjoys their interest. "Are they pets?"

"No," Peg shakes head emphatic, "...friends." and the prickly hog does huff at Maggot's finger again, sets him loud to laugh; a light and happy sound in t' night. Peg smiles. "Come," stands, stretches brief a back and makes it crack, "...you should sleep now."

"Sleep?"

"Yes."

"But I'm not tired."

"No?"

"No."

"Children *never* are!" Sometimes there is no answer to the wisdom of grown-ups, and Peg smiles at that thought as it tickles Maggot's mind with a frown. She moves a hush about the fire, comes to where he sits and makes a bed of sorts beside the fire. Plumps up leaf, makes a pillow of moss, "Here!" and pats then the ground for him to lie down. Maggot does as she intends, such is the way of children when told by adults; lays down his head and peers up at darkness; sees the night sky pretty through gilded leaf and taloned branch. Stars dance to the flicker of a fire. And there...

Above;

A white ghost as blinks its eyes...

Huge.

Peg tucks him in. Wraps blanket tight.

Warm.

"What if it rains?"

"It won't."

"How do you know?"

"I just do," Peg smiles; and in that instant sleep steals him away.

Like magic!

Peg
Chapter VIII Verse V

Pa drives fast.

Too fast.

Wheels scream, worlds fly by. A brickbuilt station where trains did stop, pretty cottages of yesteryear opposite. Once they were homes of railway workers, painted pink and blue, white, yellow; paint flaking now, forgot. The road there climbs a short hill where Pa turns sharp o'er a bridge away from the town; fears those as chase might live there. "We're getting away!" the Lady from Upstairs laughs excited, looks hopeful by Maggot on the back seat where he holds tight to the door.

Pa grins.

Eyes in a mirror...

It seems they are.

Laughs.

On the far side o' bridge, Pa throws the car sharp to the right again, sets wheels to scream and follows a narrow lane as runs alongside the railway line leading south. Stone bites through ground where dead are buried, before tall banks and unkempt hedge close tight on either side. Leaf and grass, branch, earth kiss at glass. Scary close. And on they bump, bounce, grind car o'er pothole and drain. Frightened is Maggot thrown this way, that, on the back seat; holds tight to door, eyes wide and face to window as buildings blur by. Quaint cottage, whitewashed walls of farm, and flat paddocks; wet, sodden and uninviting between them on t' road and rail built high. On the other side, fields roll up to the wooded slopes of a hill as towers tall and green, closes ever in on them as they follow the lane. But its views are shortlived, disturbed by Maggot being thrown as a rag doll, this way, that, up and down by the bounce. Catches glimpse of a train as smoulders, black carcass on t' tracks, starved horse, ragged goats, chickens, and all the while the high revs of an engine. A sharp bend to t' left; wheels screech, scream then at an impossible turn to the right. Pa does lose control to an explosion of sound: breaking glass and crunching metal, the loud cry of a horn, and then…

Darkness!

A moment, an age; then comes the return of the horn.

Incessant.

On and on as a door next to Maggot is dragged open. Metal scrapes metal, scratches ugly, a screech of nails on chalkboard, and smoke fills the air. Smells hot, ugly and of oil. Maggot lies footwell, thrown there by the crash, and the Lady from Upstairs pulls him out., drags him by an arm, bright yellow her coat. Pa still sits the front. Blood runs down about his face, rivers as fall from off his chin, and he holds tight to the steering wheel. Pale he looks to Maggot, his door buckled, trapped by a stone wall and tree. "GO!" he shouts, Pa; "GO!"

And they do.

Run!

Uphill.

"GO!" Maggot shouts, sits up.

Firelight flickers soft. Embers spin and Peg sits opposite, watches him quiet and asks soft, "A dream?" Maggot nods. She smiles soft, understands. Wrinkles her nose affectionate; "Go back to sleep now," she whispers gentle, "we'll go look for Pa tomorrow."

"Really?"

"Really," she nods.

"And t' Lady from Upstairs?"

"And the Lady from Upstairs," she smiles, "I promise." Maggot nods, eyes heavy. Believes Peg and sees the hedgehog curled up small and tight in the folds of his blanket. Smiles and strokes it gentle. Funny it huffs 'fore he lies back down. Peg smokes her pipe, and he closes eyes; feels sleep steal him stealthy away. This time though, but for the whisper of a breeze in leaf, the soft snore of a hedgehog, his sleep is deep, dreamless. Peg makes sure of it; keeps 'mares at bay.

General Pretty

General Pretty
Chapter IX Verse I

'Tis fickle thing.

War.

Knows no master, holds no faith. Men do think to control it, but they never do. Forever try. War does do as it will, and in the winds of a storm, the Tempest, it builds frightening quick. Fierce flames fanned on high. From ivory towers Monsters watch, dress pretty as Generals, eat bread, drip honey, fan flames with silvered spoons. Medals glint on puffed out chests, hang pretty from ribbons fine; colours of blue and green, red, white, gold, and purple velvet, soft to touch. Exquisite. See fingers stroke them brave. So brave, they are. Epaulettes rain from shoulders, silver and gold, buttons polished to catch the glint of light. Pretty they dance. Handsome. Sash and sword, pistol belt and whips, their household colours bright; wear them proud and strut as peacock, hen. King and Queen, Prince, Lady, Duke, Lord, they rule their lands supreme. Command, with voices loud do own the world, and the world owes them:

Everything!

So it is they fan the flames and join the storm, build the fires higher. Ever higher, 'til night is as day, day as night. Flames, wild, light dark a sky as chokes with smoke. All o'er the world, armies march to war. Hold high gun and sword, spear, stave, pitchfork sharp. In ship and by tank, lorry, boot and hoof, they will fight fierce, cruel, for Monsters as own the land, pay them to do battle and are sent in to fight; men, women and children. In town and city, village, field, forest, by sewer and through swamp, they will fight and die.

Kill.

But war.

'Tis fickle thing.

General Pretty
Chapter IX Verse II

Voices sing.

Hate them,

Fear them,

For they will take what you now have!

Chant.

Hate them,

Fear them,

For they will kill you and then laugh!

March, cross country, take cities and town, and it is the Respectable as lead from the front. Proud they are, happy, certain, sure. Grey suits swapped for the colours of Monsters, manicured nails carry a weapon of choice, and they wear their uniforms with pride. Jack boots and belt, insignia flash, wave flags and sing song. March, sing, they sing and march. Rape, pillage, torture, kill and loot any o' the Commons as dare rise against them. Pay traitors. Recruit fools. Give silver pieces, thirty each, a rich reward. And loud they sing.

March.

Hate them!

Armed with blade and bullet. Bellies fed. Clothed handsome by the Monsters as watch. Men and women, children, sell their own souls and t' souls of others for the thrill of a kill, the reward of a medal, a silvered promise of Monsters. They betray the Commons, their own kind, only now the Commons see that betrayal. Stand tall and cry loud...

FREEDOM!

And they are many.

So many.

General Pretty
Chapter IX Verse III

In city and town, village, hamlet, furrows of field and damp of fen, they stand tall, the Commons. Too many to count, too many to tell, they ignore rules imposed by the Respectable, the borders built tall by Monsters. Ignore the hate inspired and taught, link arms instead. As one. No longer are they divided by the cry of country, continent, they are the heads of corn as stretch gold in fields, reach from one horizon to t' next. In number unending they swell, men and women, the young, old, children as walk, babes in arm, they fill the streets; run as rivers and become a sea.

Swell.

Dark...

As waves. Ocean deep and fathomless. Truth-fuelled and therein a desire for justice, retribution, freedom, and equality. They will not lie down. Not again. Will not listen to Monsters and a song, the words the Respectable sing; become instead a prophecy fulfilling. As one they take up pitchfork and spear, sharp axe, blunt club. They steal the guns of enemies and roar out loud:

Freedom!

For that is what they want.

Freedom!

Know they have not the means of Monsters. No uniforms or medals on pretty ribbons, no whips, none of the Respectable to carry out their orders, sing songs, indoctrinate the lost, the floundering. They have no silver to sway the corrupt, to buy the souls of their own kind, of others; know too they have not the steel of tank nor hull of ship, flight of plane and bite of bomb. Know they are outgunned, must fight for all they have, but so too do they know they have things that cannot be bought.

They have belief.

In strength of mind.

Morality.

The steel of heart.

And might.

In numbers.

For they are legion, and war is a fickle thing. As dark waves huge, deep, unending, the Commons crash against enemy ranks, throw their own bodies against their defence. Again, and again, over, and over, in city and town, village, alley, street and sewer, in the fields by fen, in furrow, they fight and die by the hundreds of thousands, turn land and sea, the rains to red. Swell and rise again. Charge. Scream and kill. Kill and die, and for every ten, twenty, one hundred or two as die, one of the enemy falls with them. In bloody hand they lift new weapons, hold high the fallen flags, the severed heads of enemy and charge on.

A sea.

Dark.

Never-ending.

Drive back the arms of Monsters, wash clean the world in blood. Black smoke perfumes the air from fires as lick at sky, and from ivory towers the Monsters watch helpless. See armies fall and flee. Run. Rout. And always the sea swells the closer. Dark waves as might not be stopped. Monsters scream out loud in rage, frustration, stamp boots and gnash teeth helpless. Fine uniform of General Pretty, rich glint of his medals, useless against such onslaught. Monsters cry. Weep. Sob soft despair; see them fear the flames of a storm they themselves did fan and build. Make. Gates are closed, drawbridges drawn, walls of high towers manned, and helpless do Monsters watch as isles are made of their world. Kingdoms made and country kept. Cities fall, town and village, field, fen. See now the Commons lap dark 'gainst the walls of towers, surge and sing. Roar. Cry.

FREEDOM!

And believe it.

Galley Hill

Galley Hill
Chapter X Verse I

Dawn, and Maggot wakes to a white world.

Not snow.

Ice. A hoar frost is fallen from out clear sky, paints world a magic place. Leaf, bark, branch and bough, twisted root and brambled thorn, sting of nettle, fan of fern and darkest rot are all turned to vestal white, purest hue. And above, as if to frame that white, accentuate her purity, there is not a cloud in the sky.

Blue it shines.

Bright.

Cold.

Birds fluff up feathers, sit warm. Squirrels wrap tails 'bout chubby bodies. Scamper. Bound. Bounce. Nibble nuts hid clever for just such occasion. And yet for all the ice, the frozen trees and leaf above, the freezing cold that is, Maggot lies warm, snug as a summer's day 'neath a blanket in the hollow. Warm as toast. Still the fire cackles. Spits and laughs at untold jokes. Snaps loud as logs fall and embers dance, but even the fire don't explain the warmth he feels. Peg sits quiet, same as she did when he fell asleep. Pup-pups her pipe and watches him intent, green eyes bright, a-twinkle, smoke a billowing cloud of white in the cold. She smiles a greeting, "You slept well."

"I did?"

"After your dream," she nods. "Slept an age. Must have needed it." Maggot sleepy-nods; smiles and blinks bleary, rubs eyes. Sits up slow and yawns. "Come," she encourages, rises, "eat this…" takes up anew the wooden bowl and spoons hot porridge from out cauldron. Thick it steams, hot it smells, and Maggot does wonder when she made it. "It'll keep you nice and warm, wake you up." Maggot nods, sits back to log and takes the bowl from off her, yawns a "Thank you."

Peg smiles welcome.

Nods.

Retakes her seat and settles in to watch.

It tastes nice.

The porridge...

Thick and milky, hot with honey, and, as he savours the taste, he takes in anew his surroundings. Sniffs. It looks different by daylight, the Hollow. A shallow bowl in a forest of oak. White trees tower, iced of bough and leaf, circle the natural ridge about where they sit. One, though, is different from all the others.

A giant yew, black of bark and huge of girth, rises behind Peg and throws wide eaves out. Twig and branch, needled leaf, is as a sheltered roof, and small berries glint there red 'neath icy coats. In an old trunk carved by time, here and there, low, high, dark holes of different sizes; from man to mouse they gape, beckon the adventurous inside, for there might lie the way to other worlds. Even as Maggot studies the tree, the fox, as lay Peg's feet last night, does creep from out a hole at the base. Low to the ground it slinks silent. Sits quiet beside Peg and with gilded eye does study Maggot. Absent-minded does Peg stroke soft its mane. Maggot licks hot porridge from off his spoon.

As far as he can see, the Yew is the only tree of its kind. All else is oak. Giants, but somehow small by compare. Iced foliage circles the hollow. Acorn, cups, leaf, as run white away into the distance. Trees no less impressive on a normal day, but beside the yew they pale by compare. She is of the first trees, ancient and eternal, a queen among them as gentle rules. True and just, she is home to Peg, the animals of the forest. To the fox with golden eyes and squirrels as nibble nuts. To the birds in branch, fieldfare and waxwing, blackbird, starling, and the rabbits as burrow down 'bout roots, mice as hide her gown. Peep out. Maggot's eyes stray then to the giant owl as sits its perch apart. Black eyes blink slow. Deliberate. Watch Maggot bored. Beautiful she is, a visitor from another world, and Peg follows his eyes, smiles secret and whispers, "Blodeuwedd."

"Blodeuwedd?"

"Her name," Peg nods up at the owl.

"She has a name?"

"Of course," Peg frowns a grin, "we all 'ave names. It's what marks us out. This," and she looks then from owl to fox, ruffles up a red mane loving, "...is Spriggan."

"Spriggan?"

"Uh-huh," she kisses the fox's head, "...he steals butter for me."

"Butter?"

"Best butter!"

Maggot laughs, eats another spoonful of hot porridge. Nods to the lump as hides small 'neath blanket beside him. "And the hedgehog?"

"Grumpy."

"Grumpy?"

"It's not 'is real name," Peg explains, "but it's the one he lives to."

"Lives to?"

"Touch him."

Maggot does. Careful. Gentle touch, and in response a grumpy huff is harumphed from out beneath the blanket. Maggot jumps a shock, laughs happy and echoes, "Grumpy!" Eats a last spoonful of porridge and licks the bowl grateful clean. "That was *deee*-licious!"

"Good," she grins, rises, smiles; takes bowl from off him and lays it down on the forest floor, as she did the night before. Excited mice investigate. Sniff, and snuffle, do squeak disappointed. Peg stands tall, looks down to where Maggot sits. "Full?"

He nods.

"Warm?"

"Uh-huh."

"Good." She nods then, chews stem of pipe thoughtful, deliberate, and rolls it expert o'er teeth. Sniffs. "Spriggan," and she strokes fox's ear, "has found something strange."

"Strange?"

"Yes."

"What?"

"I don't know," Peg frowns concern, "...something to be seen."

Galley Hill
Chapter X Verse II

Quiet they walk. Peg. Maggot. Follow Spriggan through a world turned white. Bright the fox's fur, red and warm against the cold, and he leads them out the hollow, through a wood of iced oak to where the summit of the hill stands tall. At that top, a rise, the ground is open, the colder for being so, and sky stretches blue and broad above. Here, ice does freeze the world pretty. A tapestry. Fine webs of spider glisten intricate, silvered filigree, thin, delicate, and from nettle hairs, bramble thorn and awn of grass, ice partlets drip as precious metal poured o'er the world by Gods above. It is a world cast silverwhite. Footsteps.

Crunch!

Or at least Maggot's do.

Break frozen grass, fern frond, fallen leaf with a snick and a snap, one as warms heart with a smile. But so too does he notice Peg's feet make no sound. As the softest whisper of a summer breeze she passes, stranger for it in a frozen world. As a dream. Even the fox, Spriggan, makes more noise. Together they cross the summit, thread a way back down to trees where a narrow path circles hill. A holloway, fine and thin, worn by a thousand lifetimes of feet. High up, it looks out o'er the wooded slopes as fall steep away to t' south, and far below, as far as an eye might see, to south and west, east, low ground does stretch away to the horizon. There is a world of fertile field, flooded pasture, and lake all turned to ice, a mirror as reflects the fallen sky. A sight to take the breath away. Maggot stops to stare, a moment as Spriggan hurries on, follows path. "Come," Peg smiles, takes Maggot's hand warm in her own and follows a bushy tail, "Spriggan takes us north."

"North?"

"To Galley Hill…" she nods.

"Galley Hill?"

"You'll see."

Spriggan scampers on, stops every now and then to make sure they keep up. Follows the narrow trail as it rolls precarious down about the hill, descending as it goes. To their left the ground falls steep away, an oak forest as flows down to a dry gorge, whilst to the right, the summit of Peg's Hill rises ever higher above them, silvered fern and bracken covered slopes too steep to climb.

On the fox leads them, tongue lolling eager, down to where the narrow holloway joins the dry gorge below and becomes a wide valley through hills on either side. There Spriggan stops. Galley Hill it is as rises to t' north, opposite the hill they've just descended. Steep sloped and sheer, flat of top, an ancient fort it was. In ages long gone, there was the home of blue-painted tribes; of druid and bard, witch, warrior, and warband, and it is there, where the valley does follow its base, that they find the Lady from Upstairs.

Galley Hill
Chapter X Verse III

Blue of eye.

The Lady from Upstairs.

Maggot did not know but sees it now; quiet it stares from out pale face, the blue dull against a crust of ice as coats her skin. She still wears her yellow coat, stained red, and her other eye is gone, pecked ugly from out the socket by black shadows as haunt her feet. Large shadows as take flight at their approach.

AR!

They scream. Shout angry at being disturbed.

AR ... AR!

Beat wings thunderous loud and stall slow up into air, fly to the top of Galley Hill and watch on safe from there. Their passing – the ravens – make her swing slow above the ground, sets the branch and rope to gentle creak. Hangs ignoble from an oak for all to see, beaten bad, the Lady from Upstairs. Face bloody, bruised cruel 'neath that film of ice. Nose broke, teeth taken. One boot is missing. A rainbow sock hangs long and loose, its colours bright against a white world, and the yellow coat hides what little modesty is left to her. Not though the innards as have been cut from out and left to drop on the ground. Red and raw they are, blood froze dark to glass. It is what the ravens did feast on. Peg holds tight to Maggot's hand, squeezes it loving, and Spriggan sits quiet beside them, cocks head pretty. Above, on Galley Hill, a chorus of raven shout and scream, sing loud that the Lady is…

DEAD!

Beat wings.

There are no tears. Only a sadness.

Civilisation

Civilisation
Chapter XI Verse I

Civilisation does not fall.

It crumbles.

A slow decay as picks up pace. Plague, war, violence, death, all do ravage the land, the world, its kingdoms, continents. Erode all as is, as was, as sure as the sea does eat at shore. About them all, a storm none might now control. Stop. Rains fall, winds howl, wild and angry. Cruel Tempest as serves only fan ever higher the flames of war, spreads far the seed of plague. There is nowhere safe, not now. No escape, no far-flung corner of the world as does not suffer. Helpless do Monsters watch on. Cry. Weep with their faithful – the Respectable – servants paid to man the ramparts, sellswords from out the Commons, a love of violence upon them. In ivory towers they wait, isolated, lost in a furied sea as rages dark about them. There is no song now to win the Commons over. Instead, from towers, Monsters cry:

Oh, woe is me!

Wail:

I might now die,
Not in my sleep,
Oh, woe is me!
No wealth to keep.

Eat bread.
Drip honey.
Watch civilisation fall.

Crumble.

And fix make-up in reflections on silvered spoon.

Civilisation
Chapter XI Verse II

Without a Monsters' song to keep them shackled, the chains unseen now broke and minds corrupted freed, the Commons rage as riled sea. They want their freedom, equality, justice, want all that was kept from them. They want retribution. Sing of it. Loud waves of bloody colour as paint the walls of ivory towers, hammer on their gates and sing of death. A promise to those inside. Some towers break, a few, become a fortress fallen, walls breached, gates shattered. The Commons surge a tide inside, and from afar the other Monsters watch. Bear witness.

See.

Heads spiked bloody.

Worse.

Cry.

Oh, woe is me!

Silvered spoon a curse.

Bread crumbles.

Honey spills.

Oh, woe is me!

And the Commons cheer, sing of death. Surge determined 'gainst any walls as keep the Monsters safe. But that is not the worst of it. An enemy to all, unseen, creeps anew upon the battlefield. He is Cousin to Plague, Brother of War, and Lover of Death. Uncared for do fields fester, the harvests left to rot. Corn and wheat, barley, rape, beet, all die on stalk, roots wither in the ground, the leaf above. Potato, turnip, cabbage, and pea cast out an ugly scent to perfume the colours of death and dying, sickness, plague, and war. See the fruit of tree turn to black. Apple and pear, plum, lemon, grape, more are left to bird and wyrm. The animals in pasture are slaughtered needless, taken by the seas as angry surge, the armies of men must feed stomachs as rumble loud and hungry. From out shops and store, warehouse, market stalls, and aisle, all the food is taken, stolen, paid for, killed for; hoarded and eaten by sack and by pack, tin, can, bottle and box. The shelves are emptied. Left bare. And there is naught to replace it. Those of the Commons as pick fruit, bring in crops, load lorrys and drive roads, are no more. No men and women to bake the bread, stack the shelf and catch fish, tend farm. They fight now. Or hide. Kill. Or are killed by Plague and War.

Only now the two evils are joined by a third of their kind. On black horse he rides, stallion huge with flowing mane and nostrils flared. Hoof stamps, t' storm does howl anew, and a cruel Merchant does ride among them. Canters careless o'er battlefields, by plague pits, notices not the stench and measures instead the value of bread against weight of lead, of gold, of life, for hunger, starvation, Famine, is a curse of all men. Young, old, Monsters, Commons, minions cruel, those as hide and fight, the sick, the healthy, noble of heart and cruel of thought, all might starve, for neither freedom nor gold might be eaten.

Famine

Famine
Chapter XII Verse I

Maggot plays the floor in their front room. Small cars on imaginary road, cows as sit fields and moo. Loud a tractor grumbles, churns earth and spills mud. Maggot makes the noises. Drives intent, then pauses; nibbles happy at a biscuit safe in hand; one the Lady from Upstairs did make. Came down with them on a hot tray straight from oven. *"Baked a good batch,"* she laughed, *"...and stole t' flour."*

Food.

It tastes nice.

Biscuit.

Buttery.

And in the front room they talk as Maggot plays. Pa and Lady from Upstairs. Serious talk, in whispers quiet, look to wall and window as if someone might be listening. "There's no food left," the Lady says, and Pa does nod a heavy sigh, "I know." Maggot sniffs, nibbles; sees Pa frown annoyed, sit quiet and sip hot water from a mug. An oft-used teabag colours it weak. The Lady from Upstairs whispers on, "There's some sayin' they're eatin' dead."

"You think it's true?"

"I don't know," Lady frowns, "but we ought t' leave, just in case."

"Leave?"

"You suggested it."

"I know," Pa laughs bitter, "but it's dangerous."

"And staying 'ere aint?"

Pa has no answer. Looks to where Maggot plays their feet anew. A cow drives a tractor. Stops. Brakes with a loud *'Brmm'*, soft screech. Climbs down to say hello to another cow. They kiss. Like Ma and Pa used to. Maggot sniffs. Looks up at the quiet and bites biscuit. Sees Pa smile sad and grins back happy; returns to business of cows. *'Brmm!'*

"Tonight then." Pa decides, agrees, "we go tonight."

Yellow Coat

Yellow Coat
Chapter XIII Verse I

They leave her where she hangs.

The Lady from Upstairs.

Maggot comes to call her Yellow Coat, and sometimes, in days and weeks, long months to come, he visits her. Sits feet and wraps grass idle 'bout fingers. In and out. Roundabout. Tells her of everything that has happened. Shows her a necklace of acorn made, given him by Peg. It keeps him safe, unseen in the forest, like a ghost. And he tells her of how Spriggan, a fox, did teach him how to ring the bell of foxglove; a sign to warn others in the wood of danger. Maggot likes the old fox. Tells her all about him, and always she listens interested. Tells her too of how he misses her biscuits. Quiet she swings. Gentle in t' breeze.

Yellow Coat.

Only when all the flesh is taken, eaten off bone by bird and beast, flies black, beetles grey, the white worms as crawl and wriggle - his namesake - as Peg does take her down. Gentle, tender, they collect the bones together, wrap them up in her yellow coat, and Maggot helps. Collects ivy to tie the bundle tight together.

"Where we takin' her?"

"Somewhere safe."

"Where?"

"To Hecate, the Goddess."

Maggot nods solemn, thinks she must be someone nice if Peg and Spriggan like them; holds a finger to ivy for Peg to tie knot. Reverent, they carry the Lady from Upstairs back to the hollow. There, Peg sings soft o'er coat and bones, sprinkles earth and water, wood of yew and wolfsbane atop the remains, colours the coat with ash, and all the while Maggot watches wondrous. Listens to Peg commit a restless soul to sleep. At the end of her song, Peg gives the remains to Spriggan, so as to take them to the Goddess, and as a whisper the fox disappears into a hole in the Old Yew; it's the last Maggot does see of Yellow Coat.

Yellow Coat
Chapter XIII Verse II

On that first day of discovery though, standing in the icy cold, her blue eye dead as watches him, sadness fills the air. It joins the hungry shout and song of raven dark. Hungry on Galley Hill. Maggot knows not how long they stand there in the sadness, in the noisy silence, but it's Peg who suggests at last that they look for Pa.

Pa...

In the cold he shivers. It's all Maggot wants, all he needs, and yet he flinches at the thought; wants nothing more and fears naught less, a sickness that twists ugly inside. He looks sad and tearless to the Lady from Upstairs. Sees only the pain and fear, tortures she knew at death, and with one eye it seems she crys for him. Weeps. Tears as melt and run slow down o'er an icy cheek. A dead eye as sees innocence lost, for Maggot knows in his heart what they might find if they look, yet still he nods.

"Are you sure?"

Slow, difficult, does Maggot tear dark eyes away from the body as swings, sees Peg frown unsure. Gentle she smiles, a way out offered; a return to the hollow, ne'er to look for Pa, and Maggot might take it.

Could...

Answers brave instead.

"Yes."

Peg nods. Does take tiny hand.

Stratford

Stratford
Chapter XIV Verse I

Quiet they leave Galley Hill, the Lady from Upstairs, behind. Peg leads the way, follows dry gorge 'twixt hills downslope, and holds tight to his hand. Only once does Maggot look back. Alone she swings, a bright shadow in a white world. Black ravens hop noisy 'neath her, beat ragged wings about her. Hungry they feast. Eat. Peck at innards and shout out triumph. Maggot wonders idle if she's cold.

Sighs...

Turns away.

Smiles down at the fox as stalks his ankles. Low to the ground is Spriggan, gilded eyes and pointed ears alert to danger. But all is quiet. Ever so. Peg's hand is warm in his, hot even, like a summer's day. It warms body and bone, even as they pass by shivering oak 'neath bluest sky, earth and ground, fallen leaf and loose litter an icy crunch beneath them. Walk quiet back the way they came until, instead of following the narrow path that breaks off and makes for summit of Peg's Hill, she steps off the trail and follows the rough ground as cuts steep down through the land; follows the dry gorge as separates Peg's Hill from Galley Hill.

All about, as if asudden, a forest crowds in close. Green darkness colours the icy light, the blue sky glimpsed brief and fleeting through foliage. Careful, they must choose their step, so steep is the slope by rock and root, made the more slippery by frost and ice as carpets the world. Very air is colder too. Freezing. Breath billows as a white cloud about them, rises slow up through iced branch and frozen leaf. Maggot lifts his chin to watch. Blows biggest cloud and sees it dance a maiden fair. With a spear she fights a dragon cruel, its wings beating, long tail awhip; sees it writhe clever 'bout trees, breathes fire as wisps of fog, and whispers: "Do you see it?"

"I do," Peg answers, lifts chin to watch.

"It's like magic."

"So it is."

And, with a breeze, the magic is gone.

Spriggan scurries by, jumps on a large stone and sits pretty, bushy tail a fiery fall tipped black. The stone he sits is huge. Worked by man, dug by pick, and smoothed by hand, an age it has been there. Round of edge and moss-covered, ivy grown, nature does work to reclaim it. And it's not alone. Brethren, kin run off in two directions, the remains of a wall as was. To north and west it follows Galley Hill, keeps to the trees and bracken on that slope, 'fore it disappears from sight; and to south and west it follows the dry gorge on down the steep, keeps the wilds of Peg's Hill away from an old cottage and its garden. It might have been pretty, once.

The garden...

But it is long since overgrown.

Lost.

To brambles and nettle. Twisted and barbed, cruel thorn, sharp bite, they glisten beautiful, turned to ice by frosted fingers. Through claw and talon, the snick of sting and wasteland of hate, the remains of the cottage are broken and bent. Black bones and charred bricks as break ugly up through bleak edge of a Wildwood. In a tell of time, years not decades, it will be forever reclaimed. Become forest once more. But it is not to the cottage that Maggot points excited, "Look," he grins at chance discovery; sees rounded stone laid out low and neat, and states then the obvious, "...a wall!"

"Aye," Peg nods knowing. "One as was built by t' Lodge."

"Lodge?"

"Big house atop my hill."

"I didn't see it."

"You will." Peg wrinkles nose, studies stone, "Pitts did border their land wi' walls like this … to show they own it." Thoughtful she studies the top of the wall; looks off in both directions and takes in the lie of land; points downslope to south and west. "You musta run up my hill this way," follows the wall downslope through trees with a finger, then moves her arm in a sweep to take in the steeply wooded slope on their left, "…climbed up hill on this side o' wall."

"Why?"

"I'd not've found you otherwise."

"Oh," Maggot nods, "I see."

"And this wall," she explains, "does leads down to Stratford."

"Stratford."

"Hamlet. As follows t' lane." She sniffs a thought, points along the wall as borders Galley Hill then, "And to t' north, that way, is the old cemetery, and you did say you saw gravestones from out window."

"I did."

"So, you had to come this way…" Peg draws an elegant line in a wide arc, follows an unseen lane down through Stratford; to where the low wall they stand next to runs downslope and meets with tarmac at bottom of her hill. Maggot looks down through the trees, follows the wall with his eyes, and Peg drops her arm, whispers soft, "If we follow this wall, we might find your Pa."

Maggot nods, understands what she says. "Is it far? To t' bottom?"

"No."

Stratford
Chapter XIV Verse II

Silent they stand, stare down along the top of that broken wall as it falls slow away downslope. White and iced it is where frost is fallen. Sharp pinpricks of ice on stone, moss, black mould, the gilded spores as would reclaim it. Where cold could not reach, where nature is yet to bite, ironstone shows as dark shades of black and red. Together they stand, Peg and Maggot, Spriggan too; stand the edge of woods and of knowledge. Their next choice will decide the fate of it, for good or for bad, and in that knowing the fate of a small boy.

Of Maggot...

An age they stand.

It seems.

Quiet in the noise of a wood. Branches creak. Iced leaf cracks loud, stirred by an unfelt breeze and whisper of the Sídhe. Where a cold sun warms treetops, drops of iced waters fall, bounce off branch, onto leaf, strike floor as acorns falling heavy. Spriggan jumps down from off the stone, disappears alone into briar and bramble, would explore the old cottage. Magpies laugh somewhere in the distance, and closer to hand, 'neath sounds of silence, faint is the chatter of goldcrest and coaltit, a robin, red of breast. Yet in all the ambient noise as is, all seems silent, still, unmoving. A moment cast forever in time. Maggot looks unsure to Peg. Beautiful she is, tall beside him, trees whisper white backdrop, and as a Goddess she stands.

Slender, as a tree herself. Ageless, untouched by Time, old as rock 'neath feet, new as the hoar frost fallen, and she is of all things; of the sun and the moon, light and warmth, the cold and dark; a wonderment only a child might see. With green eyes she smiles gentle on Maggot; caring heart and soft lips, long hair the shadows of night, and she feels the fear he feels inside; asks. "Do you want to go on?" Maggot nods uncertain, unsure, whispers soft, "I think so." Peg waits quiet, gives time; sees child decide, determine fate with mind made up. "Yes!" he nods, nods again, "Yes, I do."

Stratford
Chapter XIV Verse III

Together they follow the remains of a wall down to the bottom of Peg's Hill. It is steep going, rough ground, and they slip-slide through tree, by briar, o'er root before they come at last to where the old stones meet road. There, at the end of the wall, is the bend where Pa did crash, the end of Peg's domain. She might go no further, does warn Maggot beforehand, but it does not matter, for there at the bottom is Pa.

Flies.

An angel...

Dark.

Both hands are nailed cruel above his head, thick iron spikes driven through flesh and bone, hammered deep into the wood of a telegraph pole. Alone the pole stands on the corner, marked with the number '6' and as a watcher of the woods, stained dark to keep it weatherproof, it marks where the boundary wall turns sharp to t' south and follows then the lane; marks out the base of Peg's Hill. How Pa died might ne'er be known. Dragged from out the car, bones broke in leg and arm, his flesh is cut and mutilated for fun. Ugly. Cruel. Even then he might still have been alive when they nailed him to the post. Set fire to the car beneath him, its metal...

Twisted.

Black and broke. Thick smoke as was does stain the pole, stains Pa too; feet and lower legs melted, his body, arms, head, and face burned to raw, red to black 'neath frost as paints him white. His is an agony frozen forever in death. Sculpted, as if of ice. Only then does Maggot cry quiet, tears on cheek, but for himself?

Or Pa?

He does not know.

Starvation

Starvation
Chapter XV Verse I

Starvation is cruel creature.

Sly!

A sneak as might not be escaped. There is no wall as might keep it out. No thick drawbridge or gate to close and bar, no portcullis to drop, moat to swim, no towers tall enough to keep it at bay. There is no song to sing, no heart to sway, no way to win it over. It simply is.

Or is not...

And its enemy - food - might not suddenly be grown. In a world as fights battles cruel, warfares bloody, in a land ravaged by Plague and hate, all the food is eaten. Consumed hungry by sack and pack, palette, box, crates of salted meat and cured pork, fresh vegetables, ripe fruit, grain and the grit, all has been eaten. Used to survive. Taken, stolen, killed for and gone. And with man and boy, woman, girl, old creatures, young, swept up in a war to end all wars or dying ugly in beds from a sickness none can see, no one has replanted and restocked the land. There is no seed sowed, no cow milked, no crops in field, no shoots in furrow. Nothing to gather and pack, sort, sift, butcher, spill. Nothing to transport. No sack or pack to stack shelf and feed towns, citys, the people. There is nothing. Naught. Land lies barren, fields forgot, barn and silo empty, the farms abandoned, on fire.

See them burn...

Shelf, shop, larder, pantry, all are bare. Empty. There is nothing, for greed is stupid and Man is greedy. Food dwindles, disappears, and, in its absence, starvation comes to stalk the land. Famine. A touch felt by all; a silent drum, loud in the ears of all who suffer. Monsters weep hungry, desperate, starve; no different now to the Respectable as serve or Commons as surge wild about the walls. There is no honey to drip, no bread to spread, only a spoon to admire their reflection. And when desperation dances, anything might be eaten.

Starvation
Chapter XV Verse II

Animals are first. Every animal as can be reached. In field and by forest, hearth and in bed. Cow, horse, pig, chicken, duck, and deer, the sheep on hills and wild birds o' moor, anything as might be trapped, skinned, plucked. Rabbits of warren, badgers of sett, the fox, polecat, pigeon, and wren, until it seems the very wilds are empty of life. Even ravens fly scared away from Man, and so they turn to pets. From out lap, by warmth of fire, they are taken.

Snatched!

Animals beloved. Family. Cats and dogs, hamsters, rabbit, pretty birds in gilded cages, all cooked o'er fire. On spit. Boiled as broth. All eaten with relish. Stick thin fingers suck at bone, spill juices, drool out mouth, through teeth, o'er chin, and for the shortest time their hunger is sated. Stomachs groan, cramp painful, too thin to enjoy the fat and meat, grease. Starvation turns its wicked grip. Cruel is the pain of food and full stomach, 'fore hunger returns. Too soon a belly rumbles, rolls, bangs drum, and more desperate do people look to vermin. They hunt dirt for mice, skin rat, eat insects, grass, beetles black, the worms as writhe. Anything.

Until...

At last, they cook the flesh of Man.

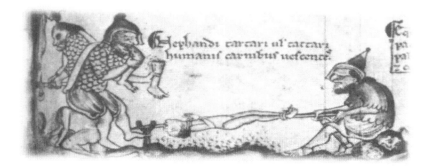

Starvation
Chapter XV Verse III

It is an evil act.

Desperate!

Wrong.

Deplorable!

No one knows how it starts. No one knows who starts it. Might be in a single place or thousand at once, by folk of the Commons or the cruel minions of Monsters. It might be the Monsters themselves? None know for sure, but start it does:

Cannibalism...

Somewhere, someplace, someone eats human flesh. Takes that first bite. Part of a thigh, a fleshy buttock, rib, or eye, eat the dead first; the dead killed in battle. Those run through by spear or shot down lane, in house, atop barricade, for none will eat victims of Plague. Even a fear of starvation does not overcome the fear of sickness. And so, at first, they partake of the brave.

Eat...

Cook them. Spit them. Roast and broil bones. Dead warriors of the enemy first. Then their own. Until, starving, they turn on the wounded and the weak. The strong do gather strength about them, and together they begin to hunt the weakest. By town and in city, 'cross field, forest, fen and firth they hungry hunt. Bands of men and women as roam the countryside, once of the Commons, forever starved, always desperate, and in ivory towers, Monsters do much the same. Hunt the faithful up tower, down stair, corner them frightened in grand rooms extravagant. Keep them caged, eat them warm. Flesh as bread, blood as honey, with silvered spoon they eat.

Survive.

Fight enemy at the walls, though now they are little different.

Magic

Magic
Chapter XVI Verse I

Tears stop.

In time...

Always.

In time...

And they ne'er take Pa down from where he hangs. Not for a lack of desire. Maggot wants to, tries, but cannot reach. Too small, even as he stands atop t' black and twisted remains of the car and does balance there precarious. Asks Peg to help, only she points out (again) that the pole and Pa are beyond the base of her hill.

Just.

"It's not far," Maggot sniffs, wipes nose on sleeve and climbs down off bonnet. Paces it out to show her. Three long strides from where the pole is buried deep aside the lane, to where Peg stands t' other side of the low and broken wall. Desperate he looks to her, pretty-framed by canopy and trees as climb hill behind her. Subtle shades of grey and green, golden brown, 'neath white of frosted ice. "See?" Maggot sad implores, cheeks still wet, eyes ashine. Peg frowns, the more helpless for how close it is, "I can't."

"Why?"

"I's bound to t' land ... land this side o t' wall."

"What's that even mean?"

"Means I might never leave my hill, not this side o' veil."

"But why?"

"Magic."

Maggot sees then, understands, for all children know that magic is alive, in everything. Children see it. Hear it. Feel it in everything that is. They know it's in the sun and the moon, in sky, clouds, the tallest tree and smallest shroom. It's magic that makes cat's tail twitch, birds fly, dogs bark and cows moo. Magic is everywhere. In hedgerows, in fields, in the black shadows of an attic, and the small flickers of light as dance and spin, swirl in and out of being and change colours when it rains in t' sunshine. It is in every animal as ever was, fox and bear, wolf, rat, and mouse; in every flower as blooms, leaf as falls and rock as is took from out the land. Magic is in everything.

Even Man...

It simply is.

Grown-ups forget, not so the children. It's why the moon does stay in t' sky, heavy as it must surely be, and why the sun does rise to wake the day. In fairytale and lullaby it dances, does creep through dreams at night, and it is magic as might explain everything. It's explanation enough for Maggot to understand perfectly why Peg might not leave her hill. "Can I visit him?"

"Who?"

"Pa..."

"Yes," Peg smiles sad, "...course you can."

"Every day?"

"Often as you like."

Maggot nods. Believes Peg's word true. Turns and looks back then to where Pa is cruel displayed. Holds him gentle in eyes. Sees beyond the screams and pain, bloody torture, the fiery smoke as stains him red and black; sees beyond the white skin of ice as coats him cold, beyond the last moment of life to a time when Pa does hug Ma tight, small boy in arms, and breathes them both in loving. Maggot remembers his scent and sees him smile.

Magic!

Is everywhere.

Maggot breathes deep and cold air fills small body; the sight of Ma and Pa real in his mind, whispers, "We shouldn'a left London."

Magic
Chapter XVI Verse II

Peg says nothing, for there's nothing to say; stands her side of the wall and smiles sad at the wisdom of children. She waits there patient, quiet, until Maggot does glance her way, and then does simply hold a hand out for him to take. Maggot nods, sees hand, and looks one last time to Pa before he clambers back o'er the fallen, icy stone of an old boundary wall. Takes the hand as waits.

"Come." Peg smiles, invites, warm voice, summer breeze as wraps him safe against cold and sad; does turn with that word and leads him back uphill. Climb together, follow low wall wall back up the slippery steep, by bramble, past briar, nettle, and thorn, to a forest of oak and elm, beech and more. Leave behind the cottaged garden and ivied wall, climb to where trees hold sway. A quiet place, peaceful, of green light and whispered shadows. Through cold air, a world iced white, they climb. Clamber. Slip and slide.

Branches creak. Leaf whispers. Ice cracks, snaps, falls heavy to the ground, and unseen does Spriggan rejoin them. Sudden, and without sound, the fox is simply there, as if he's always been. Fiery ghost in a world turned white. Spriggan lets Maggot stroke brief his mane 'fore falling in behind. Stalks ankles. Runs ahead from time to time, but never far. Never out of sight. A threesome, a triptych, as climb the dry gorge steep, back to where a trail 'bout Peg's Hill does lead off toward the summit; see Yellow Coat, brief, away in t' cold distance. Quiet she swings, the screams of ravens loud, but they do not go her way. Follow instead the narrow trail and hollowed way as takes them back up Peg's Hill all the way to summit.

Cross there, open ground to the hollow; return at last to a warm fire, pot as bubbles happy, a grumpy hog and protection of Old Yew.

There…

On Peg's Hill, where t' Otherworld touches this.

Time

A Nonsense Rhyme

THERE was an old woman,
Her name it was Peg;
Her head was of wood,
And she wore a cork-leg.
The neighbours all pitch'd her
Into the water,
The leg was drown'd first,
And her head followed a'ter.

Collected from Oral Tradition;
The Nursery Rhymes of England, 1845.

Paul Jameson

Time
Chapter XVII Verse I

Time is forever a strange thing, the moreso for being on Peg's Hill. There, it seems to Maggot, a day is a month, month an hour, and long seasons float leisurely by, yet are too quick to recall. In no time the cold does turn to warm and spring rains fall. All about leaf blossoms, explodes into life. The brightest greens fill branch of oak, elm, beech and more, return the world to life. Ivy creeps clever, climbs trunk, the twisted root, and grass makes carpet anew, afresh. Ferns flourish thick, dark the colour, signs of healthy soil, and briar, bramble, nettle's sting do stretch and flex anew. Then, when all is green, other colours join in the dance, blossom, and bloom. Small bud and pretty flower, flecks of brightest paint on a wooded canvas.

White first.

Snowdrop…

A maid as bows her hooded head. Delicate. Pretty. Beautiful. All alone for a time, before she is joined by a swirl of dancers. As bright streams they flow through the forest, 'round hill. Join hands and spin together. Enjoy long days and welcome in the warmth. See there the yellow of pilewort, a carpet of bluebells. White-gold does flower the thimbleweed, gown pretty 'midst delicate pinks of sorrel and lady's smock. Bold hue of dog violet strong does take to t' floor, tall and proud among them in emperor's hue. The forest is a tapestry of colour as changes daily. Birds build nest, sing happy, add feathers to the mix, and butterflies take to air as season turns to summer.

The hill is alive.

It lives…

And magic is everywhere.

Peg teaches Maggot of it. Tells him tales long forgot. Of woodland sprites and ancient Gods, Goddesses, and of a time when t' world was still but young. Then did the First Men walk. Pure and brave, innocent of soul, they did worship her, Peg; plant oaken grove, place standing stone 'bout summit of her hill. They called her a different name then, one long forgot, and brought her children as fall asleep and ne'er do wake; the babies born to death. Gentle Peg wraps them warm in loving arms, kisses cheek sweet, and takes them with her to t' Otherworld. Innocent souls, to be reborn immortal as elf and sprite, a trick of light, giggle in the shade.

Forever to live a land of green abundance.

Happy.

And it is they as bring them food.

From out Old Yew they sneak and peek unseen by Maggot. Elf and sprite, soft tricks of light, giggles in the shade, and as ghosts in dreams they dance and laugh, play, fill up pot, and whisper in ears. Fae, she calls them.

Peg.

Her children.

Forever.

And on that hill, they ne'er do go hungry.

Time
Chapter XVII Verse II

Yet for as fast as time flies, seasons change, it seems Maggot does play an endless summer. On Peg's Hill days are long, evenings longer, and he hunts slopes and trees, fern and frond, happy with Spriggan and Peg. Learns quick the name of root and tree, of flowers as dance and insects that flutter pretty, play delicate 'bout leaf, flower, petal, soar on uplift of air. It is a time of laughter and fun, of a boy as chases tail of fox and listens to the tales of Peg who smokes her pipe:

Pup-Pup...

Gentle soothes. Fragrant clouds, she blows.

Billow blue.

Animals come out to play. To see and greet her. Squirrel from out drey, rabbits 'neath root, bring newborn kits to kiss. Cheeky they run, jump, a madness of fun and fur, of frolic as climb legs, jump feet, curl up and cuddle warm in arms. Make Maggot laugh and smile from out his soul. Badgers waddle. Bring masked their cubs. Stag and doe, the fawn with sticklike leg. Young birds test air, wing clever 'bout heads and land their shoulders. Magpies laugh, talk achatter. Songbirds sing. Blackbird, nuthatch, flycatcher, more. Dots on high, kites and buzzard scream, play chase with raven dark, ragged of wing, and every day is something new. Hoglets huff, toads puff, and Maggot comes quick to learn the names; is taught careful by Peg. Comes too, to know the hill, the lie of land, flow of forest. Walks unseen trails and animal tracks, hollowed ways worn by man in ages past. Cuts cross country too with Spriggan; wades fern, falls of grass, climbs up steep and crawls clever 'neath root, a snatch an' catch of bramble. He comes to know the hill as he might his hand.

Home.

It is.

With secret places.

To the north and west of the summit, from where the hollow bowls and warm fire cackles, a huge bite is taken from out the very rock. A cruel wound and old scar, where once a quarry was mined in ages past. Cliffs fall sudden and sheer there, deadly, to rough and rocky ground far below. At the top, trees grip to t' edge, show roots and threaten to fall. Peg says that where once was ground and now is air, an ancient hillfort did stand. A twin to Galley Hill, palisade impossible to breach. A little further north of the bite, at hill's northernmost end, Peg's Hill becomes the Warren, and there the Lodge does stand.

Huge it is.

The Lodge...

Heavy.

With secret gardens light.

About t' Lodge they wrap. Corridors of climbing rose, wild lawn, stagnant pool and paved paths cut sharp through green, the wild wood kept at bay by walls of old. Abandoned it is, the Lodge, a place turned wild. Cold and empty, dead, forgot, thick walls and tall chimney where ghosts stalk and bats fly. At dusk they take to air.

Dart this way, that. Tiny pipistrelle too fast to see, a dark magic to behold. And with them horseshoe and long-eared brethren hunt. Seek fly and mite. Do hungry feast. But it is to t' south of summit, where the hill falls steep away in heavy wooded slopes, that Maggot loves the most. Nigh on too steep for man to climb, they peer out o'er glacial lowlands far below. To the far horizons they stretch, east to west, forever south, flatlands fed by the rivers Ouse and Ivel; the green and fertile fields as once did feed a nation. There on slope's top, where the holloway circles Peg's Hill, an old bench of wood rots slow away. Maggot sits there with Peg.

Spriggan too.

Sometimes...

Looks out and imagines he might see all the way to London. Glass spires in distance, a teasing glint; an idle dream, an imagining, but no less real for it. It's there, in among the spires and reflections, that Ma and Pa did meet, fall in love, marry; there as Maggot was born. They go there often at night – Peg and Maggot – to sit bench and watch the lights of Man sparkle. As a million fallen stars upon the ground they shine, bright flecks of white and gold, yellows, blue, and red, glimpse there the soul of civilisation.

Biggleswade, Peg calls the town closest. Directly to t' south it lies, straddles the River Ivel. She points to other places too. Small villages, smaller hamlets. Dunton to t' east, Warden and Shuttleworth off to t' west. Teaches him too of the stars above. Sits bench, cranes neck, and shows him the bear and bull. Tells tales of a flying horse, the kiss of Gods. And see there – *she points* – the Lovers. Fires flare fierce in the far away, show where man fights and kills; light up the horizon with rare shades of bloody reds and sickened orange, strange haze of smoke and fire. Trace of bullets.

Fireflies...

Explosions. A long way off from Peg's Hill.

And Tide

And Tide
Chapter XVIII Verse I

Plague and War, Famine, starvation, such is a storm as none might control. Not Monsters in ivory towers, nor Respectable as hide in the cupboards with them. Not the minions as man walls, the cruel they pay to take life. Nor is there a song to sing, compose, as might chase the clouds away. Neither might Commons fight it with strength of arm, a conviction of belief, for the storm cares nothing for righteousness and equality, for love and justice, family, right and wrong. Cares naught for life. Simply rages wild, spits blood, rains tears, carries the howls of dying on t' wind.

Such Tempest cruel cares naught for borders. Flies high o'er snow of mountain. Swims depth of sea. Strides careless o'er rivers wide and lines drawn bold on maps. Does cross them all with ease and darkens sky. Blackens world. Sucks light from out the sun, a rage its like ne'er seen before. It is a rage, a hate, disdain for life that engulfs everything. The towers as stand, cities as fall. Flag of country, continent, town and village, street, house mean nothing. Tempest cares naught for family, does tear the like asunder and slakes dark thirst upon the tears, their despair. There is nothing the storm, the Tempest, will not destroy.

Foundations shake.

Tremble.

Pillars of society, of civilisation, old and corrupt, selfish, cruel, do fall. Monsters scream, loud, in fear and frustration, desperate moans of despair, and Commons roar enraged. Hateful. About them unseen, unknown, fell riders drive horses on. Stallions huge ride clouds, white, and red, and black. Plague. War. Famine. Each does twist cruel blade. Horses scream, riders laugh, celebrate and rejoice at the pestilence, the destruction, the starvation that is their gift to mankind. Laugh at what Man does quick become.

The Fool...

As turns malicious upon itself. Feasts on t' flesh of its own kind.

And Tide
Chapter XVIII Verse II

And yet beneath beat of hoof, howl of wind, drum of rain; 'neath screams of war, death, the groans of hunger, starvation, despair, there is…

Hope!

Faint it breathes.

Delicate.

See rise the Gods and Goddess of old. From out shade and shadow, 'neath leaf, by root, they sneak, peek, emerge and return to the world. At water's edge they play, in t' surf as breaks, the still fen as dark does breathe; hear them whisper in reeds, in wind, by light of moon and the sun as sets. In forests they stir with leaf. Walk, play, dance by stream, in mist, on tall mountain tops, forever loved by the Mother, by nature, they will take back all as was stole by Man. Salted sea and rivers rise.

Flood.

Overflow.

Coastlines change. Ancient dike, sea defence, overwhelmed, wash quick away. Low isles do disappear, lie of land does change. Homes are abandoned, people drown, and the lowlands flood as dark waters take back field and plain, flood inland. In the gardens of England, the green fields as were, a shallow sea returns. Kills. Fell tsunami as roars silent in o'er the land at night, sudden, from out the east. Drowns city, takes port, washes away town, village, hamlet, home and extinguishes lights forever. High on Peg's Hill they see the lights go out, hear roar the waves as flood, one after other, the tide their master. Biggleswade drowns. Dunton. Stratford, Sandy. Unseen and far afield, cities wiped from off the map. Lincoln, Norwich, the Borough o' Peter and Burgh of Edin. Newcastle. More. London drowns. Cold water takes people in their sleep. Survivors scream, make desperate for higher ground.

Flee.

Those as can't...

Most.

Do sleep a watery grave. Wetlands return to the world. Swamp and marsh. Liminal spaces. Hear soft boom of bittern dance delicate 'neath call of cannon, the scream of heron o'er ring of bell, and with the birds return creatures of tales forgot. Jenny Greenteeth, her sisters swim, take the unwary to watery graves. Hooded monks walk the drownded paths of old, do shine their lights.

Chant...

Take life.

Woods grow wild. Primitive. Green shadows thick and dark, scent of earth and smell of shroom return to haunt the dreams of Man. Black bears and giant boar roam dangerous, wolf and outlaw, villains, hunt in packs. Steal. Eat. Kill. And in t' green shadows, in the colours of the wood, return creatures of trees and stone, earth and mind. Things unimagined since t' Dawn of Time. See dryad, hob, spirits and sprite of flower and leaf, tree, thorn, and sting. Gods and Goddess of animal, bird, star and moon, the sun, and rain. Pure of soul, hard of heart, they rise immortal, walk the world anew.

Life blossoms.

Cernunnos.

Does rule once more.

Is king.

Is!

The Liminal World

The Liminal World
Chapter XIX Verse I

"Do you think he knows?"

"Knows?"

"Pa?"

Maggot frowns, looks to Peg tall beside him. She stands beautiful against a canopy of fired golds, dark red and lighter shades of dying green. Seasons turn. Autumn announces its arrival. Acorn and conkers fall from trees, dot ground, and berries pop sudden colour unexpected. Bold splash of red and white, purple, blues and black. In the wood, on Peg's Hill, 'tis time of plenty, of forested harvest 'fore the cold months to come. Squirrels forage.

Scurry...

Jump.

Hunt food as lies the ground. Deer eat shroom, bird the nut, and thrush and starling take to sky. Geese gather on water. Honk loud, a funny sound, and begin to fly south, escape the winter snows. It is a busy time, when the warm and cold do dance in step together. Still afrown, Maggot looks back to where the pretty garland floats, bobs on still water. Peg and the animals 'neath Old Yew did help him make it. All the shades of the forest. Green, the purpled reds of ivy, golden leaf and bright berry; rosehip, sloe, the polished sheen of acorns brown and conkers dark; knotted together by brown of branch and string of stem, all twisted clever together in the weave. A gift for Pa.

Floats...

Quiet on cold water. Pa is gone, remains washed away by the cold waters as flooded so violent inland, but the pole they did pin him from still stands. 'Tis pushed to angle strange by the force of waves, and the iron spikes used to nail him up still show. Beneath the surface of dark waters, just visible, the number '6'. Maggot and Peg stand the slope of the hill where waters lap now, and the old boundary wall at the base is forever drowned. "Do you think he knows I made it for him?"

"Yes." Peg nods, eyes fixed on where the wreath bobs slow.

"Really?"

"I'm sure of it."

"I hope so."

Peg smiles gentle, ruffs his hair affectionate, and for a quiet time they watch the garland float, dance pretty. Round about it spins, twirls, swirls on unseen currents of Shallow Sea. About the hill is a much-changed landscape. Here, there, close to hand, away in t' distance, low backed banks and lonely trees rise ghostly from out water. As islands they stand, tall reed and marshgrass thick about edge. Each does mark where once was higher ground, havens now for wildlife, and even as they watch an otter takes slippery to water; see too an avocet, wigeon, the tall heron as nests tree. It is a much-changed world.

Silent.

But for t' noise of nature, distant boom of gun.

"Shall we go?" Peg asks in time.

Maggot nods, takes hand. "What we 'avin' for dinner?" Peg laughs, "I don't know." And together they climb the slope through trees; leave behind a sun as sinks fiery into dark waters, tall reed, black marsh. Sets fire to garland pretty, one as floats gentle, spins. And there, in t' shadows unseen, Pa does smile; watches Maggot climb hill, 'fore soft he fades on a rippled breeze.

Monsters

Monsters
Chapter XX Verse I

For years, decades, it has been written on the wall. Painted ugly, scrawled, printed neat and dressed up pretty. Not in words alone, but as works of art created by t' Commons. Graffiti sprayed, swirling fonts of a calligrapher's pen, ink the spit of despair, tears o' lost, abandoned, poor. In blood and more they write and draw, sculpt, sing, paint, and dream. Up wall, down alley:

And Monsters learn it true.

See it...

From ivory towers, each one cut off from t' other, and all about the wild storm rages. Plague screams in howl of wind, a wail of dread, and Famine drools as rain, dark clouds as pour down despair, heartache, to thunderous beat and blinding flash of War about the walls. Towers fall – some – number untold, unknown. High walls breached, gates broke, sanctuaries stormed, and all inside are killed. Murdered. There is no mercy, no compassion shown to painted Monsters in medalled robes, the Respectable as sing their love and praise, lie and message, the cruel minions paid to protect them; all are killed. Heads spiked bloody, bodies brutalised, tortured, screams music to a Commons long abused, cheated, lauded cruel. Their hate is real. Pure. Precious. Might not be bought, and so it is the Monsters bleed.

Red.

Monsters
Chapter XX Verse II

And seeing blood, the Commons are emboldened.

Freedom!

They roar. Scream. Believe they might win. Shackles lost, chains broke, they have the numbers, belief, and see now the fear of Monsters at the sight of their own blood. Surge as cruel sea, rabid, hungry about the walls of white towers, break down gates, smash through stone, and care naught for etiquette of old, of the borders seen and unseen. The Commons care naught for the countries painted pretty on maps, false empire, and coloured flag; no more do they care for songs all carefully composed, chiselled words screamed desperate from off the ramparts at them. No more do they care for mercy, surge dark about the walls, beat hard upon the gate, and want only:

Freedom.

Justice.

Equality.

For that all Monsters must die; and with them, any as suckle to the teat. The Respectable, their minions cruel, harlots as lie with them, eat with them, sleep with them; sing songs, their lies. Blood will be spilt and there can be…

NO!

Mercy.

Must be no mercy, and the Monsters see it true. They will not be spared no matter the outcome. Be it by Plague or War, Famine, the Commons' own hand, they will be killed; only death awaits, and in all its manners, cruel, brutal. Will be shown they bleed the same colour as everyone else. Despair does take them. Bread in hand turns quick to mould, flesh green, sickly, honey drips black, a mess unpalatable, and silvered spoons so long relied upon are worthless, cursed; do mark them out for death. Monsters weep their last; know they cannot cheat their way out, pay their way out, and so Monsters will do as Monsters will; they will destroy it all. Everything.

Everyone...

Retreat to deepest cells in towers tall, to old dungeons, thick walls of bunkers readied for just such event. Collect there all the things most precious to them. Gold and silver. Works of art. Dressed-up children, heirs to all, close the doors and drop bolts. Bar themselves in and leave all others outside – the Respectable, their minions, faithful to the end, the Commons as surge cruel 'bout walls and want their blood, bang on gates and brandish spear, promise torture. Monsters sit consoles, hope to survive the weapons unleashed.

Push button.

And let loose the dogs of war.

Monsters
Chapter XX Verse III

On pale horse, then, does Death take to t' sky.

Thantos...

Joins brothers. The fourth horseman. Hooded and cloaked, cowled, cruel his laughter, the call of trumpets, sound of siren, beat of stallion's hoof the roar as shakes the ground. All tremble: man and woman, boy, girl, young and old, the sick and starving. Dead unburied point to t' sky, see him ride with cavernous eye. Plague, War, Famine, and now Death itself does assail the world.

Horses rear.

Scream.

Gnash teeth, stamp hoof.

All o'er the world a wild storm does reach excited crescendo. Unstoppered, unfettered, unchecked, a Tempest engulfs land and sea, mountains tall and rivers deep, wide desert, the muddied swamp. Fear paints faces. Tears cut cheeks. Mouths dribble insane, for in his wake does Thantos bring Hades to the world. There will be fire upon the Earth. The flight of a thousand arrows, tails bright against the sky. As shooting stars they fly, cut air pretty and promise fiery death. It is they that will melt skin, take flesh off bone, turn loving souls to shadowed memory on stone. The hearts of nations will be plucked and taken, the largest cities will fall; turned in an instant to dust and ash, steel bones melted, broke, in time forgot. Only the dead are safe from pain, and they do point. See fly the missiles of Monsters.

Of Man.

All will be destroyed.

Replaced.

By a new darkness. Long live the Whore of Babylon.

Death

Death
Chapter XXI Verse I

"Look!" Maggot points.

Together they sit the wooded bench on t' southern edge of summit. Peg, Maggot, Spriggan, the fox, at feet. It's a cold night, dark of moon, and so stars twinkle brighter for it, the Milky Way a delicate veil 'bout Night's pretty face. Peg says there'll be frost in t' morning, perhaps a freezing fog. She knows things like that.

Peg.

Did say too, just that afternoon, that snow is on its way; pointed to a halo 'bout sun by way of explanation. This though, as Maggot now points to, does take her by surprise. Pale she turns, colour stolen from out cheeks. "Look…" Maggot laughs excited, takes to feet and points to where even more stars rise fiery tailed from out the ground. Slow they rise, seem almost to stop, stall a moment, hold breath 'fore they climb on higher into the sky. To north and south, east, and west, they climb, might lift Night's thin veil to kiss soft lips. Then faster they go.

Climb.

Fly.

Ever faster.

"…there's lots!" Hurried, Peg stands, pale and scared, throws pipe to ground and takes hold of Maggot's hand. Tight she holds to it, does make him wince and look to her concerned. "Come," she hisses, pulls him 'bout bench, "we 'as to go!"

"Go?"

"Yes."

"Where?"

"Somewhere safe."

"Safe?"

"Aye!" Peg nods, lifts dress one-handed and hurries them all away, back across the summit.

Maggot looks back o'er his shoulder, to where fiery stars still rise. A glance is all, and he wonders what frightens Peg so. On they run, back to the hollow. Peg's green cloak flows a black wave behind them, Spriggan, a fleet shadow at their side and nigh impossible to see. "Run on," Peg encourages the fox, "tell all to flee!" and as a ghost, Spriggan is gone.

"I don't understand," pants Maggot breathless, wades bramble and hears snick of thorn. Underfoot, thick clumps of grass threaten to twist ankles, and a lick of nettle burns. He wonders why Peg ignores the trails they usually take, makes straight o'er the summit by the shortest route possible. Cranes his neck as only a child might. Far above the fires rise, touch stars already there, and as pretty birds fly. Fiery tails streak bright across night sky. This way, that, impossible for him to follow without losing feet and falling clumsy. Maggot looks back to where the oak grove rises dark about the hollow ahead. Taller the trees rise with every step, underside of leaf and branch painted delicate by the warm fire as always burns there, and far above their dark canopy, a million miles away, arrows streak as shooting stars; "...why's we running so?"

"We 'as to!"

And not once does Peg let up the pace. Not even as they scurry up o'er top o' bank by grizzled oaks. Down into the hollow she pulls him, ignores the fire and their seats, black pot, its stew. Makes straight for the Old Yew.

Death
Chapter XXI Verse II

On Peg's Hill it stands.

Old Yew...

A small red berry as once was. She is of the first trees, ancient and beyond memory, careful lifted 'twixt fingers fine of an immortal soul and planted. She is Peg, and Peg is the tree. Born 'fore Man did set foot upon this land, Old Yew did see seas rise and fall, remembers the giant glaciers as carve out stone. Huge cliffs of white ice, seemingly forever, but then does witnesses their retreat and a return of warmth. A second coming, she is given life, planted by the Goddess upon a hill.

Peg's Hill.

Grows.

From seed to sapling. Young. Lithe. A pretty tree. Grows ever the taller, spreads green arms high to touch at sky, digs dark roots deep to kiss of stone; for Old Yew is a way between worlds. 'Twixt them she is. Caresses soft of heavens above, kisses unseen the kingdoms below, and brings them all to the here, to the now, to...

Her hill.

Old Yew. A doorway. A portal.

Peg.

Is worshipped a Goddess by t' First Men; as hunters they stalk and creep, as wanderers follow the lines of ley and find Peg upon her hill. Tall she stands among them, bright light of life within, and she teaches them of the trees and the woods, of animals, their ways, of the berries that grow and nuts as fall; shows them the changing moon and path of stars, the seasons. Teaches them how to live rich in ice and snow, to harvest heat of summer and love the rains of spring, the fall of autumn, and in return they worship her. Plant groves of oak about the hollow, raise stones and dance for Old Yew. Believe in her power and bring her babies born dead.

Peg remembers the first.

A girl.

Tiny. Silent. Wrapped careful warm in fur, but cold and blue 'bout lips. Peg cries, weeps, is gifted the child by a mother in hope, a father distraught. Gentle accepts and cradles her cold. They kiss her one last time, 'fore Peg takes the child into Old Yew. Travels up trunk, 'bout branch, a warm rustle in leaf as descends a shiver down through roots in a circle of stars, comes at last to an Isle of Apples; a place of bounty, health, eternal youth, and a land of many names it will become.

Tír na nÓg...

To some.

The Promised Land...

To others. And there is a child reborn. Nicnevin is her name. Fae immortal, a sprite she is and Queen she will become. More do follow. Babes born sad to death and delivered by Peg back into t' arms of life. So many names. Titania. Mab. Ainsel and Puck. Hag and giant, sprite, wisp, elf, pix', they are mischievous souls painted by good and by bad, each one reborn immortal. Forever to live in the darkest of shadow, by light of a moon, in glint of a star or giggle of wind, they are immortal. Some choose to haunt this world, most choose others, but always you might hear them laugh and play. Echoes soft, gentle, sweet, and cruel, they are ruled by love or hate and are forever children. Innocent.

Death
Chapter XXI Verse III

In the hollow, all is confusion.

Animals...

Everywhere. Hurry and run. Snuffle. Fly. Scurry from out forest, by tree. Never has Maggot seen so many. Creatures of night and day, too many to count, and all make desperate for dark gaps and openings in Old Yew; disappear inside.

Rabbit and wolf, mouse, stoat, weasel, pheasant. All together, o'er the low banks about the hollow they scurry and run. Hedgehogs huff, crickets jump, butterfly and moth do flutter; birds and squirrel hop the branch and rustle leaf, bats do flit as shadows in the night, and all do disappear inside. Badger and bear, polecat and weasel, and even as Peg pulls Maggot by the fire, he sees worm and spider, beetle, bug and slaters writhe squirmy 'bout the roots, do wriggle inside. Maggot pulls up shocked against Peg and stops the run. Worried by the panic, eyes wide, he whispers, "What 'appens?"

"We 'as to flee."

"Flee?"

"Hide."

"From what?" and even as he asks, the night does turn to day...

Bright.

An explosion.

Behind and to the south. Blinding. A pillar of fire as reaches for the heavens. Without a word then, Peg lifts Maggot, picks him up physical and carries him into Old Yew through the largest gap. Over shoulder, Maggot sees fire block out stars, and Peg whispers his ear. A spell. In a strange tongue she sings, and it is as if they are of the tree. Climb at once to t' highest leaf and swirl there in the wind, descend wild circle of stars to t' roots and rock below. Ride waves of time and space; see dark there the light, a sea as roils, and flee the fires that chase, a world as melts.

A Rhyme from out the Future

I am the King!
Said Maggot.
I am the King!
Said I.
I am the King!
Said Maggot.
Today I will not die.

Collected from Oral Tradition;
From off the Greensand Ridge.

Illustrations

Illustrations were important in the development of 'The Life of Maggot'. Here follows a list of those used within the covers, illustrations and images that helped define the story.

Cover Art: Front - Bodleian Library Oxford, Medieval Manuscript
              Butterfly Chasing (Altered Image)

Cover Art: Back - 1861 Death as a Jester by Charles Bennett
              (Altered Image)

Page 4:   1555 – Olaus Magnus – History of the Nordic Peoples
              Witch Summoning Storm (Woodcut)

Page 5:   1555 – Olaus Magnus – History of the Nordic Peoples
              Strange Effects of Lightening (Woodcut)

Page 11:   Circa 1300: The Cloisters Apocalypse
              The First Horseman: Plague (Altered Image)

Page 13:   Bodleian Library Oxford, Medieval Manuscript
              Butterfly Chasing (Altered Image)

Page 16:   Circa 1665: The Black Death in London
              Lord Have Mercy on London (Woodcut)

Page 19:   1523-1526: Hans Holbein from the Dance of Death
              All Men's Bones

Page 21:   Circa 1500: Devil Plays the Pipes on Martin Luther
              Anti-Reformation Propaganda

Page 23:   Circa 1300: The Cloisters Apocalypse
              The Second Horseman: War (Altered Image)

Page 25:   Circa 1244-1254: Old Testament Miniatures
              Joshua's Final Commands (Altered Image)

Page 27:   1612: Henry Peacham from Minerva Britanna
              'Silvius'

Page 31:   Circa 1500: Hours of Henry VIII
              The Taming the Tarasque (Altered Image)

Page 33:   1643: English Civil War
              Parliamentarian Propaganda (Woodcut)

Page 36:   1644: English Civil War
              Parliamentarian Propaganda (Woodcut)

.

Printed in Great Britain
by Amazon

21797395R00072